KISSES, SHE WROTE

Also by Katharine Ashe

I Married the Duke
How a Lady Weds a Rogue
How to Be a Proper Lady
When a Scot Loves a Lady
In the Arms of a Marquess
Captured by a Rogue Lord
Swept Away by a Kiss

Coming Soon
I Adored a Lord

Available from Avon Impulse
Kisses, She Wrote
How to Marry a Highlander
A Lady's Wish

KISSES, SHE WROTE

A Christmas Romance

KATHARINE ASHE

AVON**IMPULSE**
An Imprint of HarperCollinsPublishers

EPub Edition DECEMBER 2013 ISBN: 9780062229892

Print Edition ISBN: 9780062229908

JV 10 9 8 7 6 5 4 3 2 1

To all those who give generously from the heart.

Dearest Reader,

Once upon a time there was a castle fit for fairytales. In that castle lived a noble prince, his shy sister the princess, a count who was soon to become a duke, a governess who was soon to become a duchess, and a devilishly rakish earl who was fond of making trouble for them all. This is the story of how that devilish earl came to lose his heart to the shy princess.

Before we proceed, however, I must tell you that at the outset of this story the count and the governess are not yet duke and duchess, yet by its end they are (without much explanation here because that's another tale altogether, told in my novel I Married the Duke).

And so now without further ado I give you a Christmas story of secret desires, gallant deeds and the greatest gift of all—love.

> *Wishing you a very merry season of joy,*
> *Katharine Ashe*

CHAPTER ONE

Brittany, France

It wasn't every day that a man discovered himself to be the hero of a virgin's secret diary. So when it happened to Charles Camlann Westfall, the Earl of Bedwyr, he paused not merely to appreciate the moment but to savor it.

He came upon the diary quite by accident. Searching for a deck of cards had never proven so fruitful, even on his winning nights. Far now from the gaming hells of London, moldering away in his cousin's chateau in Brittany, he had spent the rainy day wandering restlessly, seeking diversion to relieve the tedium of too many weeks passed in a single place. Or perhaps merely the wrong place.

Paris was beckoning, specifically Madame Venus Serif, the prettiest little buxom blonde with whom he'd had the pleasure of becoming acquainted after her beastly husband lost to him at cards and demanded she relinquish her ruby necklace to pay the debt. The necklace turned out to be a family heirloom, and when Cam called on her the following day to return it, Madame Serif turned out to be rather tired of that family. Specifically, Monsieur Serif. With enthusiasm she welcomed the necklace to her breast and Cam between her thighs. Gratitude did tend to make the ladies . . . *grateful*.

That was six months ago and he'd been thinking it high time to renew the acquaintance, briefly, upon his return trip to London. That, and he'd another call to make in Paris of even greater importance. Until moments ago he had eagerly anticipated the relocation.

Tucked into a narrow compartment of a side table in an upper parlor, the diary had been barely visible. Unaccustomed to resisting his desires, Cam pulled it forth.

An unremarkable thing bound in simple cloth—much like its author—its pages revealed a stark dichotomy between external appearance and internal content.

The diary belonged to the Princess of Sensaire. During the three weeks in which he and she had both been guests at the Comte de Rallis's chateau, Cam supposed he must have seen her writing. He certainly saw her reading often enough, her nose buried in a book while her ladies in waiting gossiped and flirted.

Even if he had not recognized her penmanship, the pages told eloquently of their author's identity.

I am plain.

From the opening folio, the hand was without adornment, like the book and the princess both. The prose was equally bereft of frills.

My hair is dull and dark yet not dark enough to be exotic. My nose is long yet not long enough to be striking. My mouth is wide yet my lips are not full.

She was honest. No surprise there, though. He'd got that impression from her conversation—conversation that had required her a fortnight to manage successfully in his presence.

Though he had experienced it plenty in his nine-and-twenty years, Cam took no pleasure in the awkwardness of shy women. Indeed, he had little to do with them. Despite what his cousin Luc believed, Cam did not particularly care to hear himself prattle on endlessly. He preferred actual dialogue, even with women. Timid ladies tended to stare myopically, blush and grow taciturn around him, so he avoided them.

But for a sennight now, the Princess of Sensaire's tongue had unwound sufficient to function when she was in his presence. She seemed sensible, well informed, and probably too intelligent for him.

He turned the page.

I am tall. I have no curves or décolletage and my shoulders do not taper. I am constructed like a boy, yet I am twenty years old and female. Nature has been unkind to me. But it is foolish to rail at Nature when nothing can be done about it.

She was wise too, and refreshingly dispassionate, despite being both twenty and female.

But where I am dispiritingly mortal, he is godly. His brow is noble, his jaw strong, his cheek worthy and his nose patrician. His mouth is beautiful both at rest and

in motion, his lips sublimely contoured, his smile daz-
zling. His eyes are the color of fertile earth, the richest
brown and often sparkling with deviltry. His hair is
tawny and thick, like sun and gold. His figure is brac-
ingly manly, from his broad shoulders to his long legs
to his strong, supple hands.

It was at this moment that Cam thought perhaps to
close the diary, return it to its hiding place and forget that
he had ever come upon it. He knew what he looked like; he
saw it in the glass and heard it upon his lovers' lips open
enough. To hear it stated in quite these terms was another
thing altogether. And he had never been privy to praise con-
cerning his hands from a lady upon whom he had not used
them.

It made him a little nauseated.

But perhaps she did not in fact describe *him*. Perhaps she
had at some other time encountered a blond-haired, brown-
eyed man and considered that poor fellow godly. Cam flipped
back to the initial page. The date at the top read 4th September
1817. The day after he had arrived at the chateau.

He folded the diary closed and considered.

It would be the height of dishonorableness to continue
reading. The princess deserved her privacy. Merely because
she was writing about him gave him no right to read it. On
the other hand, weren't ladies supposed to keep their diaries
hidden beneath pillows or locked in dressing tables? A girl
silly enough to leave her private thoughts displayed so bla-
tantly in a plain notebook tucked snugly in the back of an
undistinguished piece of furniture in the corner of an out-of-

the-way parlor frequented only by her closest female companions deserved to have her privacy invaded.

He continued to invade. The next page was dated 7th September.

> He walks with confidence yet ease. He speaks without any appearance of forethought yet his speech is pleasing, amusing and clever. He dresses with elegant ostentation yet carries it off as though he wore the lowliest peasant's garments.

Now that was going a bit far. He had the self-presentation of a *peasant*? No peasant he'd ever seen wore a perfectly starched Mathematical and an antique gold watch fob, nor boots that shone even after a lengthy ride.

> I believe it is a lack of conceit. He pretends to be conceited and has every reason to be: he is an earl and extraordinarily handsome. But now, after observing him for several days, I do not think his apparent ennui and general nonchalance spring from a lack of care about others or a too-great fondness for himself. I think that is all a sham. From the clues I have gleaned from my governess, Arabella, he would not have aided her journey here if he did not care for others greatly.

> Too intelligent, indeed.

> That care he has for others—not his masculine beauty or title or wealth—is what makes him godly.

Well, she'd finally got one thing wrong. After this little jaunt to France, he was nearly broke. The princess might think him godly, but here on Earth, merchants, not to mention the men one played cards with, expected to be paid what was owed them.

The renovations on Crofton had not yet taken root. Like his wastrel father, Cam was no natural farmer. But he had done his best to improve the West Country estate he inherited nearly a decade ago, and he'd had modest success. When his new steward suggested changes, he welcomed them. Now he'd barely a shilling to spare. Haring off to the French countryside had been as much to escape the temptation to spend money on game and women in London as to bring Luc the news of their ducal uncle's death.

Crofton would turn around within a year. Or two. He hoped. Until then, a French chateau on his cousin's penny seemed as good a place as any to dally. That wasn't, of course, the only reason France appealed to him of late. But it was useful.

Now, however, he had a princess with a hero-worshipping infatuation to address.

They were an exceedingly modest party at present: the princess; her brother, Reiner; the princess's beautiful governess, Arabella, whom Cam had conveyed hither; and now his cousin Luc, the Comte de Rallis, as well. Also in residence were the princess's four ladies in waiting, all of them happily married to Reiner's courtiers and therefore uninteresting not to mention probably off limits. He'd known Reiner since they were youths, and a man owed his closest friends some consideration, after all.

A modest party indeed, which would make it difficult to

entirely avoid the star-struck girl. The infatuation, however, could not be allowed to flourish. Cam didn't typically care about what others thought of him, but now that he knew what Reiner's young sister had been thinking he really should put period to it. A man could only bear so much undeserved adulation.

He stared at the book in his palm and pondered his options.

He could become raging drunk and embarrass himself in some publicly horrid fashion that would leave her glowing notions of him trampled. He hadn't got that drunk in years. It would be uncomfortable and leave him with a wretched headache. But it might serve the purpose. Females were remarkably squeamish.

Or he could simply take the diary to her now, let her know he'd read it, and watch as she dissolved in embarrassment then threw the book dramatically into the hearth. Sheer mortification. Shame and anger. End of infatuation. Mission accomplished.

Trouble was, the Princess of Sensaire didn't seem the type to dramatically throw treasured objects into the hearth. She seemed too rational for that. Cam generally found rational females to be hardheaded. The wealthier they were, the more hardheaded. She might respond to a direct approach by digging in her heels.

Whatever he did, it bore further consideration. He should probably at least glance at a few more pages. For inspiration.

12th September 1817

Because I am not beautiful, he does not look at me with appreciation in his eyes, but as though I might

be another man or a servant or nobody. He is gentle-
manly. I find no fault in his manners, but his appreciative gazes are reserved for attractive women. He
looks at my waiting lady, Mme. Desere, who is wonderfully pretty and has an enviable bosom, with obvious appreciation. He looks at Arabella in quite the
same manner, but although she is very beautiful, his
appreciation of her seems rather more general, even
brotherly.

The princess was observant. And Cam's mild nausea was
back again. When had he become such a cad?

I am shy. I am an unwilling conversationalist. I am
bookish. I would rather write than flirt. I prefer
walking outdoors and riding to dancing in a ballroom. Maman chastises me for this. I know she is
right.

A frisson of sympathy ticked him. Dreadful parents were
a curse no young woman—or man—should have to bear.

I do not blame him for not noticing me in particular.
But I should like it to be different. I should like for
once to not only be a princess but to feel like a princess
too. I should like to be showered with the attentions
of a wonderful man.

And so, since I am not treated to his appreciative
glances during the day, I will treat myself to them at
night. For where his attention is held by beautiful

ladies in the drawing room and dining room, in the
privacy of my bedchamber he will be mine.

Well. All right. This was interesting.

One night soon, when the fire on the grate has burned
low and moonlight illuminates the bedclothes, I will

Footsteps sounded in the corridor. Cam closed the diary,
slid it back into its nook, and crossed the room toward the
door. Hands clasped behind his back, he smiled as though
it were simply a rainy day at the chateau and he was simply
wandering aimlessly, searching for diversion.

The Earl of Bedwyr appeared in the parlor doorway and a
little puff of breath escaped through Jacqueline's lips. Predict-
ably. Over the past three weeks she had lost so many breaths
that if she were a superstitious person she would fear she'd
already given up her soul.

She should have long since become accustomed to him.
But after writing the newest entry in her diary, her cheeks
wanted to hold heat more ardently than ever. It had left her at
once buoyant and peculiarly agitated.

"Ladies." He bowed beautifully—always so beautiful.
With his slightest gesture, her insides fluttered like caged
butterflies. With his smile, they clenched like the sweet grip
of a hand within.

Arabella curtseyed. "My lord." She was reserved with
both him and the master of the chateau, the Comte. Any

servant would be reserved with noblemen, after all, even the finishing governess of a princess. But Arabella was also beautiful, just as the earl and the Comte were. So were Jacqueline's ladies in waiting.

She was a wren among peacocks.

The corner of Lord Bedwyr's mouth curved upward and his gaze shifted to her. Her throat went dry, her hands damp. *As always in reality.* She could bring nothing to her tongue. Except in her diary. In her diary she teased and tempted, her voice softly husky as though with fire smoke, and he was mad for her.

"The rain seems to have diminished," he said. "Shall I escort you ladies about the garden? We will all dampen our shoes and become uncomfortable and irritable. But we will have each others' company and that will elevate our spirits." Eyes the color of deepest autumn did not waver from hers. Indeed, he looked at her now for longer than Jacqueline had ever had the distressing pleasure of enduring. An odd, hot delight gathered in her middle.

"My lord," Arabella said, "her highness must assist her majesty to make the guest list for the ball to be held in two days."

"A ball?" He did not remove his attention from Jacqueline. "Capital idea. May I inquire as to the occasion?"

"To celebrate the Comte's return to health," Jacqueline said, because she could reply to a simple question directly addressed to her even when addressed by a god—albeit thinly, as though her breaths were insufficient to carry the syllables. "He has been recovering from an illness."

"Ah, yes." His gaze slipped to Arabella. "For some weeks now."

Arabella abruptly moved away. "Do come along, your highness. Her majesty must not be made to wait."

The earl watched her depart, his regard vibrant. There was some mystery between these two, Jacqueline sensed, some secret that made Arabella prickle with mistrust when the earl spoke to her. The Englishwoman held her feelings close, though, and Jacqueline hadn't had the courage to pry.

Then Lord Bedwyr stepped toward her and concern over Arabella's moods fled. The nearness of him and awareness of her perfect inadequacy submerged her again in despised silence.

She struggled to meet his gaze, managed it, and did not flinch. After all, sixteen hours earlier she had made him beg to caress her. *In her diary.* But his eyes were not now swimming with desire. Instead, he studied her quite like a Man of Science might study a specimen, but one that sincerely intrigued him.

"You are a dutiful daughter," he said, surprising the quiet that had settled around them in the cool dampness of the castle's interior.

"The ball was my idea," she said because, except in the pages of her diary, she could only ever tell the truth.

How many untruths did this man tell the women he seduced? Her waiting lady, Madame Bernard, said the earl's many conquests—all of them—were married. Such a man must make women many promises he did not intend to honor to encourage their infidelity.

He bent closer. "Fond of dancing, are you, your highness?"

"Fond of celebrations, rather," she replied, tumbling into his scent. It was not what she expected—costly Eau de

Cologne—but sage and perhaps a hint of leather. "It is a great pleasure to amuse one's friends with entertainments."

"Ah, then you are simply fond of pleasure." At any moment his gaze would slip to her long nose, her imperfect brows, her pointy jaw, and he would remember with whom he was speaking—not alluring Madame Desere or lovely Arabella, but plain Princess Jacqueline, his friend's timid young sister.

"I guess." She *guessed* she liked pleasure? Oh why, *why*, couldn't she be the teasing temptress of her fantasies?

But what was to stop her from being that now, alone with him here just like in her diary? She blurted, "Who isn't fond of pleasure? Certainly you are, my lord. You never cease teasing my ladies in waiting. It is as though you wish only diversion at all times."

He lifted a brow. Before he could speak, her tongue hurried forward. "Or perhaps you merely have nothing else to say to them. Why is that, my lord? Don't you know how to read?" Oh! Speaking to him like this was *delicious*, even if she uttered the words somewhat haltingly so they sounded more peevish than coquettish. That she uttered them at all was a triumph.

He grinned slowly. "Moderately well. The question is, do they?"

Jacqueline could not hide her satisfaction. "In truth, I have never noticed it. So perhaps they prefer teasing to substantive conversation and you are doing them a great service."

"The world is too full of unhappiness, princess, for a soul not to seize every moment of enjoyment and savor it." Then his gaze did slip down to her lips and rested there.

As misery curled in her stomach, his brow creased.

He backed away a step. "Off to your guest list you must go now," he said lightly. He bowed and with an elegant flourish of a wrist from which peeked a hint of the most understated lace, he gestured in the direction Arabella had gone.

He wore lace cuffs. In 1817. When no man who valued his manhood wore lace cuffs. And yet those cuffs did not compromise one jot of that manhood. Rather, they proved his confidence. No wonder she was infatuated.

Jacqueline curtseyed. Without waiting for her departure, he strode away.

She went into the little parlor where she and Arabella took breakfast each day before Arabella gave her lessons about what to expect of English society. She was to be fully prepared when she, Reiner, and their mother visited London at Christmastime.

She understood her brother's intention: to secure for her a husband. A decade ago Reiner had been to university with the young lords of England, men like the Earl of Bedwyr and the Comte de Rallis, heir to the duchy of Lycombe. Honest, noble and honorable, a titled lord of Britain would make a valuable ally for Reiner's mountain kingdom and a fine husband for the sister he held in great affection.

Moreover, their mother insisted. At twenty, Jacqueline was already years past the age she should have wed. But she and her brother enjoyed each other's company and he had not yet himself thought to marry. Now their mother was making her intentions clear: by year's end Jacqueline must marry a man of Reiner's choosing. In England he would arrange a match for her.

Despite the close friendship of a decade, he had never once mentioned the Earl of Bedwyr as a candidate.

"A man may esteem another as a friend," he'd said to her after the earl's arrival at the chateau, "without wishing to curse his sister with him as a husband." No further explanation came. Madame Bernard's gossip must suffice. Lord Bedwyr was an unsuitable match for a lady of virtue.

Jacqueline had never nursed dreams of a dashing husband. Reiner would make certain she was comfortable and his kingdom well served. The fate of a princess was not her own to dictate.

Her fantasies, however, were.

Hurrying across the parlor to the little table, she drew her diary out of the tight compartment. No one had discovered the hiding place. That her pulse leaped as she opened it did not mean anybody else sensed the fever radiating from the cloth and paper. It was her secret.

Before, her diary had been the stuff of any girl's days: accounts of walks in the garden, conversations with Reiner about the kingdom, dissatisfaction over her mother's demands, notes on books she read. Then the Earl of Bedwyr had arrived at Saint-Reveé-des-Beaux. In a sort of despair born of knowing he would never look at her in the way she longed for him to look at her, her pen found new inspiration. But she could no longer record the truth. The truth was too limp and sorry a thing to flow from a princess's pen. So she made it up.

This inspiration now was acting on her like spring sunshine upon a bud. Petal by petal her soul was unfurling. Not a rose, glorious red or pink—never a rose. Instead, a tulip, simple, white, plain. Still, in her imagination, she was blooming. Proof: she had teased him!

She guessed that this nascent confidence came from the

brazen boldness she exhibited in the fantasies she penned. She didn't mind it. If pleasure could be had only through fiction, then she would happily dream.

Tucking the diary back into its hiding place, she left the parlor and went to help plan the ball at which she would stand against the wall with the matrons until Reiner found dance partners for her. But in her dreams of that ball she would dance with an earl, and he would be smitten.

CHAPTER TWO

A ride with Reiner did not accomplish it. An argument with Luc didn't either. Madame Desere dipped her fan over the deep cleft between her breasts. That did momentarily distract Cam. The invitation to join her in her chamber at night while her husband was in Sensaire, however, he declined.

Instead, restless, he prowled the house. All was at sixes and sevens with preparations for the ball. The princess's governess went about in distracted agitation. Luc was much the same. The queen was at her most imperious, the ladies in waiting aflutter, the servants frantic.

Amidst the bustle, only the princess was sanguine—so sanguine that when he encountered her before the drawing room door she did not even blush. Instead she calmly took his proffered arm, commented on the fine quality of English kerseymere beneath her fingers, and allowed him to lead her in. Detaching herself from him gracefully, she moved to the tea table with a regal glide. She was by no means a beautiful woman, but when she left off stammering and blushing, she was quietly elegant.

And that was the problem. She didn't *seem* like the sort of girl to compose invented scenarios worthy of the Marquis de Sade. But what else could she have meant by *in the privacy of my bedchamber he will be mine?* How on earth could he be hers except unwillingly? And what sort of fun would that be anyway? While the idea of ropes and chains didn't precisely repel Cam, he much preferred the free use of his hands with a woman. True, his tongue was remarkably talented. But he saw no reason to limit his lovers to less than the skills of the entire man.

But what else could the princess have written? *He will be mine.* He couldn't imagine.

Granted, his imagination was not particularly fecund at present. Once upon a time he had allowed it to thrive, back in his university days when he hadn't a care for anything. At that time the virile confidence of youth had flowed from his pen onto pages in the form of both valiant verse and puerile poems.

Then war came, his father died, and he was no longer heir but master of hundreds of people dependent upon him. When, after three brief years enjoying life without the man who had made it miserable for her, Cam's mother died, his Muse had fled. Now he was lord of a struggling estate and not even in possession of the one thing he actually did covet. Byron, the lecher, was filling feminine breasts with heat while tupping young boys in Greece, yet Cam, who was adored in boudoirs across England and France, could not force a single coherent line of verse from his pen. It was damn lowering.

More lowering had been the dashed hope in the eyes of the girl. Claire. His new ward.

She'd taken him off guard that first day six months ago when they met in Paris. Afraid of the little he had to say to a child of twelve, and even more afraid of disappointing the ghost of her mother, he had grappled for subjects to discuss. When he mentioned poetry, her eyes had brightened and she begged him to write a poem for her—in French, her mother's tongue, or English, the language of her father whom Cam had slain as the brute beat his own wife to death.

He said no. He didn't write poetry or anything else. Not anymore. Not for a long time.

Hope bruised, Claire's eyes had dimmed.

Without ideas, he could not write, even if he knew it would give his ward happiness, and even if he suspected it would give him some relief from the heavy concerns that he could not now escape even in drink, game, or feminine flesh. Simple relief in simple pleasures.

Pleasure . . .

What in God's name had the princess written about him in that diary?

Although he tried with the entire spec of honorability in him to withstand the temptation of going to that parlor, finding her diary, and reading more of it, ultimately he succumbed. The ladies were in the ballroom supervising decorations. None would disturb him. With his back to the closed door, he slipped the diary out of its hiding place and opened to the last line he'd read.

One night soon, when the fire on the grate has burned low and moonlight illuminates the bedclothes, I will open the door and he will be standing there. His godly glow will shine upon my pale ordinariness, and he will not notice the stark difference between us.

Though I am in my nightclothes, I will invite him in. He will enter.

The door will close and we will be alone. I don't know why my heart should pound like the drumming of kettles at a festival when he draws near. He has not come to me before, but I know what he intends.

Of course she knew—the timorous minx. She was inventing it. Ah, women. At once, the most painfully obvious and delectably mysterious creatures on earth.

He will touch me, and I will allow it. He lifts his hand, strong and golden, and I am bathed in his sunshine anew. It shimmers through me and brings me to life. When his fingertips brush my cheek there is already warmth beneath them. It is not the warmth of shame, but ecstasy.

Ecstasy? From the tips of his fingers upon only her cheek? Elsewhere, perhaps. But her *cheek?* Cam frowned. She was farther gone than he'd imagined.

My heart beats swiftly. Soon he will kiss me. I want it but I am confused by my fear. If I welcome his caresses, he cannot harm me. He cannot steal my soul, after all. He is only a man, not a fey prince with magical powers nor an elfin king bent upon kidnapping.

Cam's frown tipped into pleasure. She had a whimsical turn of the imagination. It bespoke lightness in her spirit that he had only begun to discern in her regular conversation.

But his fingertips caress — the gentlest caress — and I am lost already. At so slight a touch! How can I be so foolish that such a thing so strongly moves me?

At least she knew her reaction was extreme. That was a good sign.

It must be foolishness. For it is I who controls this affair. It is I who makes the demands and he who acquiesces. Here in this bedchamber I am his sovereign, and he is mine to command.

"Touch me here," I say, brushing my fingertips across my brow. He complies. Along the length of my hair his golden light lingers, clings. I lean into the caress. There is power in his touch, but I will only succumb to it at my leisure.

"Touch me here." I lift my hand, lay it palm up and trail my fingertips across it. His follow. I shiver but, contrarily, heat gathers in me. Only he has ever made me feel this and I welcome it.

I slide my fingertips across my wrist, to my elbow. "Here," I say, and when he obeys I become the heat. I become sunlight. I become beauty.

Cam closed the book. Not because he wasn't curious to know where she would demand he touch her next.

Not because some vestige of honor that after years of debauchery still lingered in his noble blood and demanded he cease this invasion of her privacy at once. Not even because his heart was beating at an uncomfortably uneven cadence.

He closed it because, like a bell ringing silvery sharp in the highest tower of the most distant church, an idea was occurring to him. At the edge of his imagination, it teased. Eyes closed, he tried to seize it. It skittered away.

He opened the book and sought the lines he had already read.

I am bathed in his sunshine anew.

He scanned the page.

It shimmers through me and brings me to life.

The idea flickered, like the inconstant flame of a candle in a breeze.

It is not the warmth of shame, but ecstasy.

Sunshine.

There is power in his touch.

Bringing her to life. Rousing her pale ordinariness to life.

"Like a statue," he murmured. "A statue in an impenetrable stone courtyard." The image grew stronger in his mind. "Stone warmed from the dawn's light glowing across the cold white marble."

He stared down at the open book. Light. But not light from the sun. A man composed of sun. A faery prince. A stone princess and a prince of golden sunshine.

> *Like marble in its stony jail that*
> *When dawn comes drinks the sun,*
> *From rigid dark of lonely night*
> *He woke her*

Cam's fingertips itched. Not to caress the princess's cheek. Of course not. As Reiner's sister, a maiden, and in no way the sort of women whose cheek he had ever considered caressing, Princess Jacqueline was even more surely forbidden than her ladies in waiting.

For the first time in years his fingers itched to compose. Ideas swirled—words, phrases, even verses.

> *Of princess born of throne and state,*
> *These humble lines will tell . . .*

> *No winsome lass of beauty fair,*
> *Nor gay of heart was she,*
> *But grey like wintry dusk, her eyes,*
> *And locks of ebony.*

> *Pale porcelain skin, not cream or milk,*
> *Nor lavish form or tongue,*

> *Nor cherry lips; a sober maid—*
> *Unused, unloved, unsung.*

> *But like boughs in Aquilon's frosted gloom,*
> *Who sleep, and sleeping dream,*
> *Awakening from stone-bed drear,*
> *The maiden*

The maiden ... *something.* All words, meter, and rhyme would come. Now only the shaping of the drama mattered.

> *The King went forth on Solstice dark*
> *And swore to Heaven*

What sort of Heaven?

> *And swore to lofty Heaven*
> *To wed his daughter by fortnight's end*
> *To a warrior full-proven.*

> *"A tournament throughout the land*
> *Mars' rough games will dictate;*
> *Clashing steel and savage arms*
> *Shall guide my daughter's fate."*

> *His Queen of violent beauty scorned*
> *Her blusterous sovereign's prayer.*
> *"What knight will have this tim'rous girl*
> *Whom I wept tears to bear?"*

> *But the proud King he vowed anew*
> *To spread the maiden's fame;*
> *A dower of castles strong and jewels*
> *Would her husband gain.*

What about the tower? A stone tower of impregnable strength, at the top of which the princess sat in her barren courtyard, in the darkness that hid her plain face, her slender body unshaped by feminine beauty, unwanted except for the wealth that attended her.

Her lack of beauty notwithstanding, she was still the same old princess, same old cruel king. The story had already been done in poetry, hundreds of times, for hundreds of years.

Not this time. For upon the eve of the tournament the story would take its turn. Imprisoned in her tower of stone, she would find a way to escape for a night.

> *They beckon through the silver door,*
> *Entwined with vines and verdant,*
> *All light and joy and laughter's glow,*
> *All Nature's beauty potent.*
>
> *"Come, princess sad, upon bright feet,"*
> *Gaily the fey entreat,*
> *"Come laugh with us, come sing and dance.*
> *Come, princess, to the Feast!"*
>
> *The mortal girl unbinds her hair*
> *And moves with steps unsure,*

Shadows bend to brilliant day,
Toward shining gate's allure.

There would be a river, or perhaps a sparkling brook, and a grove given over to the feast, and magic. The story was unfolding in his imagination. He needed only pen and paper. Shoving the diary into its hiding hole, Cam went from the parlor to his quarters. After long years, he had found his Muse.

The ball came and went. Lord Bedwyr asked Jacqueline to dance but they did not. Instead, as so often in the past two days, he disappeared before the end of the party.

It was to be expected. All was in an uproar. The Comte and Arabella had danced then quarreled, and Arabella had fled. After that the party descended into a gossiping melee.

Then Reiner told Jacqueline the truth of it: Arabella and the Comte were wed. Against Arabella's wishes, Lord Bedwyr had facilitated the hasty wedding while his cousin was unwell. The mystery of her discomfort with the earl was solved, though not the reason they had all kept it secret. But Arabella remained silent on the matter and, hiding her own secrets, Jacqueline did not press her friend for more.

The Comte and Comtesse left for England to take up his ducal inheritance. Jacqueline waved to the traveling chaise, and as it disappeared down the long esplanade of stately trees, two riders came into view.

Beside her brother, upon a stallion of creamy white, the Earl of Bedwyr made a vision any foolish girl would swoon

over. But Jacqueline was not foolish, only foolishly infatuated. She urged her mount forward. A month earlier she would not have had the courage to approach the earl, even with her brother; she would have ridden away swiftly and pray he hadn't noticed her. But late last night after the disappointment of his early departure from the party, she had lain in her bed and let him cover her with his body, and he had groaned in pleasure.

In her diary.

Her blood rushed, the fire in her cheeks never hotter. But she met him and Reiner on the drive with outward composure. Lord Bedwyr removed his high-crowned hat and bowed from the saddle. Sunlight struggling to make its way through clouds seemed to gather, drawn forth by his golden mane, to revel gloriously about him. Buckskin breeches caressed his thighs and his voice was low and pleased when he spoke.

"Seeing off the happy couple, your highness?"

"Why didn't you tell us the truth of it, my lord?"

"I was asked not to." His rich gaze glimmered.

"I think you chose not to."

"Jackie, do cease plaguing Bedwyr," her brother chided with good nature. "A man can't like that from a lady."

"I think he likes it. I think few ladies dare to criticize him and he finds it refreshing." She attempted a saucy grin. It wobbled a bit.

The earl's lips curved to the side. "You think too much, I begin to suspect."

"I think you liked being privy to the secret when others were not," she countered, unstung by his words. This w what ladies and gentlemen did. Flirted. Bantered. Until she'd never had the courage. Her diary had given it to h

"Do you?" His smile seemed fixed now, no longer amused. "Reiner, old friend, allow me a moment's conversation with your sister, will you?"

Reiner's brow went up. "Jackie?"

She nodded, her stomach tangling in knots.

"All right," Reiner said. "But if I hear you've been on anything but your best behavior, I will be very cross." He pulled his mount around and headed for the stable.

"I wonder to which of us he was speaking just then," the earl said, again with the slow smile that made her breathless.

"Both of us?" This glow in her breast was not real. It was entirely born of fantasy. But it felt remarkably good.

"I daresay." He drew his horse beside hers and his boot brushed the thick fabric of her riding habit. It was a startlingly intimate contact and she was unprepared for it. Her hands jerked upon the reins and her mare's head bobbed.

The earl glanced down at where his leg now was inches from her skirt, then back up into her face. Resisting the urge to cover her flaming cheeks with her hands, Jacqueline gripped the reins.

"Reiner said you are to have the credit for securing the Comte and Arabella's marriage," she said. "He said that when the Comte fell ill you brought her here to protect her."

"Hm. I wonder from whom Reiner heard that story. A servant, no doubt."

"Isn't it true?"

"In some part."

"The part you played?"

"Alas, princess," he said with a wry lift of one brow, "weddings have never been my forte."

"Rather, marriages," she corrected him, audaciously, outrageously, and it felt *spectacular*.

"Quite." He smiled. "Why, your highness," he said without pause, "did you wait until just before my departure to begin to—what was it your brother said?—to plague me? It is perfectly diverting and infinitely preferable to the imitation of a porridge you affected for the first few weeks of my sojourn here."

A *porridge*? This time it stung. Never mind that it was accurate and made her want to laugh aloud. "Do you depart soon, my lord?" Her heart thundered.

"Your brother intends to travel to London to secure proper lodgings before your arrival. I will accompany him and take advantage of the excellence of his hospitality along the route. Will you miss me?"

She would not miss the aching misery of longing she felt each time she came within the circle of his glow. She welcomed his departure. "Why did you disappear from the ball last night before its end?"

"What an agreeable tendency we seem to have of ignoring each other's questions," he said, his eyes hooding. The breeze ruffled the locks of hair at his collar. She could feel them, silk and warmth, between her fingers. She had felt them night after night in her dreams. "Do you think we will ever communicate anything of substance to each other if we go on in this cryptic fashion?" he said, studying her again, but a grin had settled in the corner of his mouth.

"I don't know," she said, holding her breath as if that would contain the quivering inside her. "Perhaps we could give it a try now."

"Splendid." He bowed. "Ladies first, of course."

"All right. Will you remain in London for long, my lord?"

"I have no immediate plans not to, your highness. Will your visit to London be lengthy?"

"Not above a month, I believe. We are expected in Sensaire after the New Year." For her wedding to any titled lord her brother liked except this one. "There. We have civilly exchanged information. That must be accounted communication, mustn't it?"

"Indeed," he drawled.

"We should congratulate ourselves."

"Now it's my turn."

"Your turn?"

"To ask a question."

"But you already did."

"A mere parry of yours," he explained.

"Is that how conversation in your society progresses? Like a fencing bout?"

"Usually. Silly, isn't it?"

"Sporting, I should say."

A smile of genuine amusement creased his mouth. This was real pleasure he was feeling in her company, not manufactured in the pages of her diary. Jacqueline felt as though she had gulped an entire glass of champagne.

"As an avid reader, tell me," he said, "are you ever moved to turn your hand to writing?"

"Writing?" she said upon a gurgle.

"Writing."

Of all questions, how could he ask *this?* "I don't know why I should tell you anything about myself."

"Whyever not?"

"You called me a porridge."

"Do you mind it much?"

"Yes." Her lips twitched. She turned her face away. "Not so much."

"Not at all, I suspect."

She pinned him with what she hoped was a hard stare. "How can you claim to suspect anything about me?"

He did not immediately reply. "Would you believe a little bird told me?"

"I shan't call you incorrigible, my lord, for I guess you have been called that before—"

"From the time I was in short-pants."

"—and my chastisement should fail from banality."

"Never."

"And I shan't gape at your inappropriate familiarities, for I think that would only make you say more to try to shock me."

"Probably." He folded his hands across the low pommel of the saddle, waiting, she realized, his gaze upon her warm with amused interest.

"Oh." She was a wretched liar; he would see it in her face. "Yes, of course I write."

"What sort of writing, I wonder?"

She shrugged, a habit that her mother decried as unsuitable for a princess. "Correspondence and such," she managed airily.

"And such?"

"Notes from my lessons and the like." Not entirely untrue.

"Ah." He seemed to consider. "I understand."

He understood nothing. "Why this interest, my lord? Are you a writer?"

He offered her a modest smile. "Merely a dilettante."

She had not expected this of the pleasure-loving nobleman. "A novel?"

"Actually, poetry." He said it so simply, so honestly, unlike her response to him, that beneath her ribs she felt an echoing discomfort.

"Poetry?"

"A short poem only, for my ward. A story of a princess in a castle tower. You know the sort. My ward is twelve."

His *ward*. This rakish lord had a child? Perhaps his own child by a mistress. He would have been quite young, of course. The notion poked at the discomfort in her breast like a hot iron.

"In your poem, did a prince rescue the princess?"

"No, in fact," he said, his gaze quite fixed in hers, like on that rainy day in the corridor. "Not yet, at least."

"Ah, you are sending it to your ward in installments." Her gloves gripped the reins so tightly her mare shook its head again. "That is cruel of you, my lord, you know, to draw out the suspense like that."

"I know the torture of reading a work in installments, your highness. Quite well, in fact." He leaned forward in his saddle as though he would continue. Some gleam in his dark eyes seemed to warn and question at once. Then the easy, careless mask of idle amusement once again descended over his features. He took up his reins. "Now, let us be off to the house. I promised the queen that I would play whist with her before dinner." He drew around his stallion, his body shifting so effortlessly that he seemed one with the magnificent creature. He had been in the British cavalry during the war, and she had no doubt he'd been as dashingly noble then as he was indolently elegant now.

"Whist?" she managed. "With my mother?"

"It seems she wishes to be a card sharp upon her entrance into English society, and as the resident gambler here, I am to instruct her."

"I don't believe it."

"Do you impugn my integrity, your highness?"

"I don't. I don't believe you have any integrity to be impugned." She said it lightly.

"Clever girl," he said with a knowing, sideways glance at her that tore her breath from her lungs. "Very clever girl."

Jacqueline did not weep when Lord Bedwyr departed the chateau with Reiner. A princess did not weep, even at the departure of the only man who had ever stirred any profound feeling in her, the only man who made her feel like a very clever girl not only at the end of their conversation but throughout it.

They parted on excellent terms. He took her hand and bowed over it but did not kiss it. In his eyes was pleasure of the enjoyment in each other that they had found two days earlier on horseback.

If he remained in London for the holidays, she might see him. Even so, they would not enjoy the same easy concourse they had come to so late here. In London he would not be idly seeking diversion on a quiet estate and content to find it in a plain, shy princess, but immersed again in his world of beauty and fashion.

"You needn't have concern," her mother said as she poured tea from an intricately painted pot. "Lord Bedwyr will not bother himself with you in London."

Jacqueline's cup *tinked* on the saucer. She steadied her hand. "Why should I have concern over such a thing?"

The queen's brows lifted above crystal blue eyes that Jacqueline had not, unfortunately, inherited. With such startling eyes, Jacqueline might have been accounted an Original if still far from a Beauty.

"His presence here rendered you mute for a month, daughter," her mother intoned. "Gentlemen seeking brides of worth admire modest, unassuming ladies. But a man of influence will not offer for a girl whose voice he has never heard."

Lord Bedwyr had heard her voice. Her teasing had made him smile.

"Yes, Maman."

"You must show yourself able to be a hostess in a great man's household, not a mouse."

"Yes, Maman."

"You must be prepared to lead ladies of lesser rank in fashion and taste." She perused Jacqueline's gown of virginal white with approval. Of course she approved. She had directed the making of it and every other gown she possessed. Sometimes Jacqueline wondered what it would be like to wear something not tasteful, simple or virginal.

"Yes, Maman," she said, biting back her desires. Despite the earl's departure, euphoria still ran through her like the strongest, blackest tea. He had awoken a sleeping sprite in her—rather, she had awoken it with her diary. Now it would not sit quietly and be forgotten, even in his absence.

"No matter." With a tiny silver spoon the queen stirred sugar into her tea without once touching the sides or bottom of the cup. "After your brother arranges your marriage, your duty will be to speak infrequently, intelligently and usefully."

"I believe I can manage that."

Her mother's gaze rose above the rim of her teacup. "He has found a duke for you."

This was news. "A duke?"

"Tarleton. It is an ancient family possessed of several estates in addition to the principal seat, and sufficient wealth and influence." Turning her nose from the tray of delicate French pastries, she chose instead a dried grape from a silver dish.

"Sufficient for what?"

Her mother cast her a crisp look. "Sufficient to assist your brother with the business of our kingdom." She always said "our kingdom" as if she were king, though she wasn't even a queen any longer, really. When Jacqueline had been an infant and her father died, Parliament proclaimed that no more kings would reign in Sensaire. The prince would retain his role as head of state, but if the realm were to avoid devastation like that wrought in France by Revolution, he must share power equally with Parliament and the barons. Eleven at the time, Reiner accepted the ruling of his people. The last Queen of Sensaire had bowed her head and wept in fury.

"If not the duke, Reiner has other prospects," her mother said now. "You will wed at Christmas."

So soon. October would be upon them in days.

"Oh."

The queen's lips folded into a line of satisfaction that Jacqueline had never herself been able to master with her identically thin lips, perhaps because she had never wished to appear so smug.

"I pray you, Maman, if it suits my brother, allow me to enjoy the holiday with my English friends without concern about the future." She would go to Arabella, and perhaps, one last time before she married, make the man of her dreams smile.

Her mother's face settled into its customary severity. "You can no longer run from your future, daughter. You are—"

"A princess. I know my duty. But I will still be a princess after Christmas. Waiting an additional fortnight to marry me off will not change that."

The queen's nostrils pinched.

"When the New Year comes," Jacqueline hurried to add, "I will go willingly to whomever Reiner chooses. Until then, allow me a final Christmas without care." A Christmas of fantasies.

For a moment that hung with her hopes, her mother considered, and Jacqueline knew why she asked for this; on her wedding day she would set her diary in the fire and watch it burn. A princess could not comport herself as a bride while giving herself in fantasy to a man who was not her husband.

Until then, she would allow herself to dream of beauty, pleasure and light, and to know what it was to feel alive.

CHAPTER THREE

London, England

Candlelight glinted off the goblet between Cam's fingers and set aglow the cheroot smoke that hovered about the room. The rumble of male voices in conversations throughout the club's grand chamber and the scents of wine and brandy, the savory remnants of beefsteak and onions, a dozen colognes, hair powder, damp wool and shoe polish all penetrated his senses far too acutely.

Unlike his companion, Captain Anthony Masinter of His Majesty's Royal Navy, who sat across the table with his hand upon his hip as though fondling the hilt of a sword, Cam was not relaxed. Rather, a stretched restlessness attended him tonight as it had for weeks already. Earlier he'd declined Tony's suggestion that they visit a favorite gaming parlor. At present he had no appetite for those pleasures, only this agitation that clotted his thoughts.

"Preston is glaring at you," the captain said, twining a long black moustache between thumb and forefinger.

Cam lifted his glass to his lips. Perhaps he wasn't drinking enough lately. Perhaps that was the problem. He'd been shockingly sober for most of his sojourn in France and hadn't quite gotten back up to speed since returning. But he'd felt this restlessness long before France.

"Dock Lady Preston lately, have you, Charles?" Tony said with a grin.

"Preston is a bastard."

"That's what they say. But the Dowager Lady Preston insists it is not so." A waiting pause ensued, then Tony dissolved into deep chuckles.

"It is pathetic when a man must laugh at his own quips to fill the silence, Anthony."

"No more pathetic than sitting around ape-faced for weeks upon end," his friend countered pleasantly. "If you haven't been servicing the lovely Lady Preston while her lord speechifies in the Lords, what have you been doing with your days?"

Tearing out his hair. Staining his fingertips with ink. And getting nowhere. During the journey across the Channel, the poem had flowed. But for weeks now nothing had come. Half-finished and scattered over his desk, the pages seemed to mock him each time he entered his study. Each day the verse hadn't come, his restlessness grew.

"Avoiding your inane questions," he replied, swallowed the last gulp of brandy, and stood.

"Where are you off to now? Madam Patrice's? Or Lady Preston's, given that Preston seems to be settled in here for the night?"

Cam scowled.

Tony's bright blue eyes went wide. Of course they did. Cam never scowled. Ever. Other men scowled. Cam indulged.

Perhaps that was the trouble. Too much hair tearing and not enough indulging. But he hadn't been indulging when the idea for his poem had occurred to him. He had been reading a maiden's fictional diary.

"Neither. Good night, Anthony."

Striding toward his house in long, hard steps, the sound of his boots on the pavement dampened by London rain, and the shoulders of his greatcoat growing heavy with moisture, he knew what he needed now. Aylesley. The house in which he had lived with his mother for twelve years while his father disported himself with mistresses in town would cure the discontent simmering in him, he was certain.

Tucked into a Kentish hillside along a tributary of the Great Stour, backed by the ruins of an ancient monastery, not far from a working mill, and surrounded by woodland out of which popped the neatest little village in which a boy could easily make both friends and trouble, Aylesley had been his home much more than Crofton. There, in the absence of his father, his mother had taken his education upon herself, teaching him the languages, natural and political philosophy, history and art that a future earl must master. French lessons had been attended by the finest delicacies her émigré chef could concoct. Astronomy was learned on nights upon the roof staring at the stars. And she had been his first dancing partner, he standing on her toes to learn the steps, she laughing and teaching him how to laugh, despite the heartbreak of her life.

When he turned twelve, his father had sent him to school, abandoning his mother to lonely months during which she was allowed no pleasure except when the earl called her to town to act as his hostess for a political dinner. Afterward he would banish her again to Aylesley, where in shame she hid her fresh bruises with powder. Cam visited her on holidays and they laughed and danced and watched the stars again.

He needed to go there. A month at Aylesley—perhaps two or three—would put him to rights. He would drink up sunlight undimmed by town fog, lie on the roof and count the constellations, and his poem would come back to him. Then he would have something to send to Claire to enliven her spirits. Her nurse's latest note had been grim. Missing her mother and alone in Paris, his ward was disconsolate. If only he could bring her to Aylesley.

An impossible dream. His great-aunt, who owned the house, did not approve of him. She had told him in no uncertain terms not to visit Aylesley unless he had first reformed his libertine ways. That she had also announced to every one of her nieces and nephews that upon her demise she would leave the place to Cam—the least grasping of her miserable relatives—took the edge off his frustration somewhat. But it didn't help him now.

Perhaps he should go home. But even the thought of it roused his anger. He couldn't step foot in Crofton without hearing his father's voice and hating him all over again. And at Crofton Claire would always be known as the master's by-blow, no matter that she was not. Rather, she was the daughter of a woman he'd known long before her brutal marriage, the woman who first introduced Cam to the wonders of the female body, and who years later, when her husband was beating both her and her daughter, had called on Cam to defend her.

So he had. Now he was responsible for a twelve-year-old girl.

At Aylesley he could provide Claire with a proper home, not a hired flat in Paris. Her father had been a monster, but her mother had been a lady and Claire deserved as much. Crofton was not that home, though, and Aylesley was not an option. So he would remain in town and tear out his hair.

The clock on the table in the foyer of his house was striking nine when he discarded his sodden coat and hat in his butler's hands and started toward his study.

"My lord, her ladyship awaits you in the Gold Room."

He halted. His staff only referred to one woman like that.

"She's in town? Here? At this hour?"

The servant nodded solemnly. Straightening his shoulders, Cam mounted the stairs.

Years ago one of his father's mistresses had done over the parlor in the Egyptian style with yellow silk walls and faux mummy cases. In collective denial of the chamber's hideousness, the servants called it the Gold Room. Cam rarely received at home anybody but his closest friends, and had never bothered to redecorate.

With the first words from Lady Letitia Rowdon's mouth, he wished he had.

"I see that hussy's tenure as mistress of my late nephew's house has not yet been entirely erased."

"Which hussy?" Cam said though he knew he should not bait her. Dwarfed by the mummy case beside which she stood, all wiry four and a half feet of her wrapped from chin to wrist to toes in dull ebony taffeta, and seething with compressed disdain, his great-aunt commanded the room as though she were an empress.

He waved a hand. "There were so many, I cannot be expected to remember them each individually, m'dear."

Her dark eyes snapped. "You are a young jack-a-napes, Charles Camlann Westfall."

He made a pretty leg. "You honor me."

"It was not a compliment."

"I am fairly certain I understood that." He went toward her, took her proffered hand, and bussed the tiny, claw-like limb. It always required this gallantry to remind himself that she was not seven feet tall and made of steel, but an ancient wisp of a thing he could topple with a light breath. "Welcome, darling."

She snatched away her hand. "Why hasn't one of your mistresses redecorated?"

"They have their husbands' houses to decorate, Great-auntie. They don't need mine."

"Profligate wastrel."

"I am flattered, ma'am." Gently he guided her to a chair. "Now, do allow me to pour you a brandy while you screw up your courage to tell me what has brought you to me so late of a Wednesday eve."

"Aylesley."

Lifting the brandy carafe over two glasses, he drew in a breath and poured. "How is the old shed lately? Drafty and moldy in this season, I suppose, or you wouldn't be in town."

"Aylesley is in excellent condition, of course," she clipped. "I know you want it, so don't try to bamboozle me into believing you haven't a care for it."

He tucked a glass into her outstretched hand. "I would never dare such a thing."

"You want it and you shall have it, as I've said to all those weak-chinned cousins of yours. You are carved in the image of your father, but you are my favorite niece's only child and so you will have the place when I'm gone."

"I am gratified," he murmured, the hairs on the back of his neck standing up. She was not here only to repeat this. More would come momentarily.

"I have altered the terms of your inheritance."

And there it was.

"Have you?" he managed smoothly enough.

"I will give you Aylesley now, but first you must marry."

"I haven't any intention of marrying soon, my dear." Or possibly ever. He'd at least four cousins to ensure the continuance of the line, one of them already with sons. And marriage as he had witnessed it had never particularly appealed to Cam. That, and his father—damn his soul—did not deserve to have his blood continued anyway.

She set down the brandy. "You will marry now if you wish to have Aylesley. If you do not, I will deny it to you upon my deathbed."

She couldn't. It was all he had ever wanted.

"You won't."

"The documents are already drawn up and signed."

"I will purchase it from you. Outright." He didn't know where the words came from. Desperation? He didn't have the liquid capital for such a thing, not even remotely.

She knew his thoughts. "You haven't the funds. And don't imagine the card table will supply them. Your father was just such a fool and you wouldn't wish to follow in those footsteps, would you?" Sly eyes studied him. She knew Crofton had suffered. She had him by the ballocks.

"What do you want with my house anyway?" she demanded. "Do you intend to set up your mistresses there?"

Rather, his ward.

"What I do with the place after it's mine is no business of yours," he said languidly.

"It will not be yours unless you wed."

"All right." He affected nonchalance. "I will consider it." He could pretend until she signed the deed or dropped dead of perpetual disdain, whichever came first.

"Wise boy."

"I haven't been a boy in seventeen years, Auntie." Not since his father had exiled him from the only place in the world that had made him happy, and the only person. "I suppose you have a bride in mind?"

"My goddaughter."

"Ah. I see. An antidote, is she?"

"A great beauty, in fact."

"That is good news. Are she and I already acquainted, by happenstance?"

"She is a young lady of excellent breeding and comportment."

"I am to understand that means 'no.'"

"Lady Amelia Whitley is the daughter of Maythorpe who, unlike your father, did not run his estate into the ground. He is offering ten thousand with her."

Cam whistled low. If the dowry came to him unencumbered, with ten thousand pounds he could put Crofton to rights immediately. Marriage was looking better and better.

But something didn't fadge.

"Forgive me for prying, my dear," he said, "but given the lady's manifold attractions, mightn't she find a husband without you throwing her at my head?"

"She wants the house."

A chill breath seemed to emanate from the empty hearth to scurry about his legs and creep up his spine. "Does she?"

"She adores the property. Last summer I told her I was giving it to you. The next day her father made the proposal to me." His aunt stood up to her full height of a broomstick. "It is high time you cease your libertine ways and settle down to your responsibilities. Amelia was bred to be a countess and she could be the making of you. Tell me now that you will wed her by the New Year and I will deed Aylesley over to you this instant."

This instant. It could be his, finally. The restlessness would cease. Forever.

"I will do it," he heard himself say.

His great aunt nodded once, sharply, and in tiny firm steps, strode to the door. Halting there, she turned to him. "If you do not wed her, I will give the house to your cousin Henry."

"Henry? That manipulative weasel?"

"He is eager to possess both the house and my goddaughter's hand."

"He will not have the option." He bowed.

"I am staying in the usual place. Call on me on Saturday to meet your intended. Two o'clock."

"I shall suffer your absence every moment until then, my lady."

Narrowed eyes glared anew. Then she left.

Cam walked slowly to his bedchamber where his man had set out a glass and decanter. He filled the glass, went to the chair before the hearth, and lowered himself into it.

So, he was to marry. He'd known precious little about being a school student when his father had banished him to Eton, but he had learned. He'd known nothing of war until his sojourn fighting Boney from horseback, and he'd learned that too—quickly. He hadn't any idea what being a guardian entailed until a Frenchwoman he'd spent a total of one night with begged him to take her daughter as his ward, and he hadn't yet mucked that, though if he didn't settle Claire into a real home soon he might.

With the despicable disaster of his father as his only example, he knew nothing whatsoever about being a husband. But he knew the one place in the world where he felt at peace, the one place, *the one thing* on earth he loved without measure. For Aylesley he would learn how to be a husband. After a decade of alternately avoiding or defending himself at dawn from them, at least he had a running start on how not to be one.

The dawn spread in crystal mists across the park, and the Prince of Sensaire's horse made hoofmarks in the grey frost upon the grass as man and beast approached Cam.

"You have returned," Cam greeted him as their mounts blew wintery plumes of smoke.

"Last week. Luc didn't tell you?"

"Haven't seen him. I assumed he was enjoying the benefits

of wedded bliss before he and his lady return to Lycombe for the holidays."

"They've decided not to retire to the country until after the New Year," Reiner said, coming alongside him as they headed toward the gate. "Truth is, I'm relieved. Jackie is glad for Arabella's company. With my mother pressing her to marry, she's in poor spirits."

"Ah." So the shy princess of the vivid imagination was to be married. Commiseration would be in order, except he suspected she at least would have some say in whom she wed.

"I should not have allowed this." Reiner shook his head. "If I'd found a husband for her years ago, she wouldn't have grown so independent."

The diffident girl of the first few weeks of Cam's visit to Saint-Reveé-des-Beaux had not struck him as independent. But the woman on horseback he'd spoken to that day before he left France, the woman of the quick tongue and perceptive eyes—remarkably fine grey eyes flecked with green and gold—he'd *liked* her. And her diary certainly bespoke a creative mind.

"Troublesomely independent?" he inquired.

"No. But I anticipate resistance from her now." Reiner peered at him and his high brow—clear and intelligent like his sister's—creased.

"Don't look to me." Cam laughed. "I know nothing of choosing grooms. Or brides for that matter." His was being chosen for him. He opened his mouth to say that, then closed it. Friends, even the longstanding sort like Reiner, did not need to know a man's private business.

"I don't suppose you do," Reiner said affably.

"Have the Queen and your sister arrived in town yet?" he asked and felt that perhaps the question was not as casually offered as it should have been.

If the princess were in town, her diary would be too.

"I brought them from Portsmouth last week. It is the very reason I'm out and about so early today. A fortnight ago the house was empty and peaceful. Now they've got the whole place upside down. At the command of my mother, every servant was awake before dawn."

"In preparation for the introduction of suitors into the place?"

"In preparation for Christmas." Reiner chuckled. "I say, if you haven't breakfasted yet, do come by and share mine. Your presence will allow me an excuse to decline hanging holly until after I've had coffee. My mother won't be thrilled to see you, of course. Never has liked you. But Jackie will be pleased."

"If it pleases the princess, I am at her disposal."

They shook the chill from their greatcoats and entered the royal residence to a scene of holiday activity. Footmen rushed about with armfuls of greenery, gold cording and red ribbons, and maids brandished feather dusters and brooms.

They found the Queen and her daughter in the drawing room, with the queen's personal maid.

"Lord Bedwyr," the Queen said coolly in greeting.

"Your majesty." He offered his most elegantly unruffled bow. "Your highness, what a delight to see you again."

"My lord." She curtsied with great grace. No rosy glow showed upon her cheeks, no trembling fingers clutched at the ream of crimson ribbons in her hands, and no quick breaths lifted her breasts tight against the fabric of her gown. As unlike the timid girl he'd first been introduced to in Brittany as could be, this woman stood with quiet composure in her slender frame, leveling at him a subtle yet thoroughly impenitent grin.

Impenitent?

About *what*?

It must be the diary. After he left the chateau had she continued to write about him? To what extent? Had the innocent caresses of her fantasies grown less than innocent? Even if they hadn't, would reading those entries inspire him to begin writing again?

"I found this fellow wandering in the park," Reiner said. "Don't think I've ever seen you awake before noon, come to think of it, Bedwyr. What's the occasion?"

Restlessness, now pricked with energy. "Naturally, I hoped to encounter you and win an invitation to breakfast. Not breakfast with you, of course. Your majesty, your highness, have you broken your fasts?"

"I take only tea before luncheon." The queen gestured with sharp motions to her servant toward a box of porcelain figurines. "That one, Marguerite. The angel Gabriel."

The princess's attention darted to her mother for an instant then returned to him. "My brother," she said, "is the only person of this household allowed to lie abed until all hours during this season, my lord."

"I'd hardly call eight o'clock 'all hours,'" Reiner protested.

"The rest of us haven't the leisure for—"

"Leisure?" Cam supplied.

"Escaping," she said serenely, her shoulders straight and her fine eyes direct, as though it were all the rage not to be fair or curved and she had every confidence in her ability to intrigue a man with a single word.

Which she did.

Escaping? Escaping what? Duty? Her mother? Reality? Truly, this was a new woman.

"There are boughs to be hung and garlands to be fashioned and gifts to be chosen," she said, gesturing to the open boxes arranged around her white skirts.

"Ah, gift selection. I'd nearly forgotten about that."

"Haven't you anyone to whom you wish to give a gift this Christmas, my lord?"

"No doubt I do," he said easily, an uncomfortable tightness in his chest. He hadn't a mistress currently, and he typically gave his servants three days leave and a guinea each. He gave no other gifts at Christmas. Not since his mother died. "My valet always provides me with a list of suggestions for his gift."

"That is very considerate of him."

"Do you think so? I've always thought it rather peculiar."

"But why? He seeks to make discharging your duty easier on you."

Duty. She imagined that giving gifts was a duty to him. And she was probably right.

"I believe a gift has greater effect when it is chosen by the giver to best suit the recipient." Memory stirred of the Marchioness of Dade's glittering green eyes when he presented her with a Christmas gift last year—emeralds—a surprise, like his announcement that their liaison would soon end, delivered as he clasped the necklace about her throat. The effect of that gift had been precisely what Cam intended: an enthusiastically affectionate final parting.

The glimmer now in the intelligent eyes of the Princess of Sensaire had nothing of coquettish avarice about it, however, but thoughtful interest. *Interest.* From a lady to whom he had given nothing. Less than nothing. A few unremarkable conversations. Not even flattery. Just as her diary had recorded.

"I suppose that makes very good sense," she said. "Perhaps you ought to give your valet something unexpected this year. To surprise him."

"Perhaps I will."

"Enough of this chatter, Jackie," Reiner said, moving toward the door. "I'm famished."

"Brother, at times I do not know how I ever imagined you to be the finest gentleman in all the world," she said with affection.

"I am certain Lord Bedwyr wishes to be on his way," the queen said without looking at either of them. "Marguerite, Balthazar *maintenant.*"

The princess's gaze met Cam's. Her eyes twinkled. He bowed and followed the prince to the dining room.

His appetite had fled. As Reiner read the paper and enjoyed a lavish breakfast, Cam could think of nothing but that diary. If the princess had made the subtle shift from girl to woman since he'd seen her last, her diary entries might have altered as well. What new inspiration might he find in them?

A niggling discomfort at his state of preoccupation bothered him. He could not recall the last time he had fixed on anything to the point of distraction.

At the chateau. After he'd read her diary.

He *must* read it again.

He set aside his coffee and stood. "I'm off then." No trace of frustration colored his voice. He was not entirely lost to himself over an innocent's fantasies. That gave him some comfort.

"Mother's hosting a supper party on Tuesday," Reiner said without removing his attention from the sporting news. "You'll have gotten the invitation."

A supper party? Five days hence. If the guest list were sufficiently large, he might be able to slip away without detection and search for the diary.

Good God, what was he thinking? Secretly skulking about his friend's house in search of a girl's private scribblings was below even his standards of reprehensibility. A man should have some integrity. In any case, it was impractical. In a house of this size servants were everywhere.

At present they all seemed to be on the first and ground floors. Instructing two footmen in the hanging of greenery in the foyer, the housekeeper gave him a shallow curtsey and returned to her task. A quartet of maids appeared from the rear of the house, arms laden with boxes marked *Noël*. One maid peeked coyly at him then dropped her lashes.

Cam made a mental accounting. Reiner's court had not accompanied him to London. As such, there could not possibly be more than five above-stairs maids and two footmen in the town residence of the royal family. Could there? He'd been a bachelor for so long, with little need for servants and less money to pay them, he wasn't certain. In the winter season the lovely marchioness with whom he had enjoyed a satisfying interlude employed only three maids, one footman, and a butler in addition to her dresser and the marquess's valet.

Sparing a moment to recall the marchioness's soft bosom marked with tiny scars from cigar ash with which the marquess had dusted her during a nasty tiff, Cam wondered how she was faring now. After he ended their liaison, she'd taken up with an Italian war minister, going about town with him quite openly while her husband stewed. The sweet little marchioness had even sent Cam a note, thanking him for giving her the courage to strike out on her own. He had not intended that, of course. But if she was happy, that suited him.

Another maid scurried down the stairway, trailing white gauzy fabric with a large silver star attached to it. That made six maids, all intent on decorating. Without further consideration for anything but the humming impatience in his blood, Cam went up the stairs two at a time, around the landing, and up again.

In stark contrast to the frantic holiday industry on the lower levels, nothing disturbed the midday quiet of the second story. Reiner's valet could be behind any of the doors letting off the landing, most likely in the dressing room. What of other upper servants? There could be another personal servant to be accounted for . . . Dammit, there must be. Cam never dressed his lovers after he had undressed them; he preferred to depart while they were still lounging in bed, glowing with satisfaction and feeling as though they had been thoroughly adored. Still, he knew ladies required a bevy of servants to dress. The queen probably did too, though the princess's simplicity of style suggested she would scoff at such a thing.

Not scoff. Rather, with a wry smile she would brush away attempts at over-indulgence. There was a certain graceful humility in her usual restraint, he thought.

A door handle turned. Cam grasped another and slipped inside the chamber—clearly Reiner's room, decorated simply and with an eye toward his tastes: a portrait of a hunt and a statue of a pack of hounds.

The next door let onto a chamber lined in bookshelves with a single table in their midst, several stuffed chairs, and a framed map of Reiner's mountainous kingdom. Not a chamber intended for ladies. But Reiner had never been much of a reader, yet the fire crackled merrily. The princess, of course, was well read.

The door behind him creaked open, then it stalled.

Justifications for his presence above stairs rapidly queued in Cam's mind. None sufficed.

"No," came the princess's voice from the other side of the partially open door. "I shall be only a minute."

A muffled reply issued from below.

"*Non merçi*, Marguerite," the princess said firmly this time.

Heavy russet draperies fell full to the floor at the window. Cam slipped behind their voluminous folds.

The door clicked shut and soft footsteps crossed the chamber quickly, then she came into view through a crack between the draperies. Pausing before a bookshelf, she pried forth a volume.

The diary.

As though she heard his quiet release of breath, she glanced to either side. Then, moving to a chair, she slid down into it. Her shoulders seemed to relax and she laughed.

He had never heard her laughter before. At once throaty and sweet and secretive, it acted upon him like the stroke of a feminine fingertip down his chest. He held perfectly still, measures of astonishment and chagrin mingling in him. It was best he hadn't heard her laughter in France. If he had known then that she was capable of that mysterious little alluring sound, combined with his knowledge of her diary, living under the same roof with her might have proven uncomfortably tempting.

Now, however, that was not at issue. Now he need only wait in this library until she left and satisfaction would be his.

The general disinterest with which the ladies of English *haut société* were receiving the plain and painfully shy Princess of Sensaire in London had become her mother's constant complaint. Nevertheless, Jacqueline's humor remained light; she had Reiner, Arabella, plenty of books, and her diary for company. Her mother, however, was suspicious of her spirits that remained high despite her lack of social success. Recently she'd set Marguerite to spying. Jacqueline couldn't go four yards without the woman dogging her steps.

Days ago she'd hidden the diary in the library, assuming it would be well concealed here. But after Lord Bedwyr left and Marguerite ran off from the parlor on some flimsy pretext, Jacqueline's pulse had raced. Enduring her mother's entire lecture on speaking too familiarly with a gentleman of

Lord Bedwyr's reputation, finally she was able to escape to the library.

The diary was safe. The fruits of her imagination would not be stripped bare.

No imaginary encounters with him, however, compared to reality. When he appeared with Reiner, every mote of her blood had rushed to vibrant life. A man should not be allowed to be so handsome. In France she had tried to convince herself that his godly appearance alone affected her, that the warmth in his eyes and the thoughtful cast of his brow were fruits of her imagination as ripe as the fantasies in her diary. But she had seen that depth again today, heard it in his voice, and could not believe he was the man her mother claimed.

Yes, he'd had a string of mistresses, and his lifestyle suggested a man of indolent habits. But Reiner had told her about the old earl and the estate Lord Bedwyr now worked diligently to put to rights. He'd shared the story of the earl's young ward much more reluctantly, hesitant to speak of such matters. More importantly, he hadn't heard the story from Lord Bedwyr himself; the duke had told him. For all his scandalous affairs, the earl was a private man.

She wanted to know more about that private man. She wanted to know what had driven him from bed so early on a Thursday morning, what gift he would choose from his valet's list for Christmas, which beauty of the *beau monde* currently enjoyed his attentions, and whether the tips of his fingers were stained with ink because he had been writing more poetry for his ward.

Smoothing her hand over the diary's cover, she gave a little laugh. He was still a libertine and still as far from her as the stars. And in five weeks she would be betrothed to marry a very respectable duke.

A fire already burned in the grate, chasing away the chill of the early December morning. Reiner directed that a fire should always burn here for her. The pride he took in her humbled her. He would not give her to an unkind or unintelligent husband. The Duke of Tarleton must be a good man.

She could burn the diary now and cast the earl entirely from her thoughts. Or for a few more weeks she could enjoy his company, as she had at the chateau when for the first time in her life she'd felt truly alive.

She tucked the diary back in its hiding place and nerves buoyed her to the door. Having seen him today would surely fuel her writing tonight. Nightfall already seemed too distant.

CHAPTER FOUR

The poem was no longer for his ward.

The day after reading the diary again, Cam finished the first part. The sad princess, having escaped from her stone tower with the aid of the faery people, remained in the land of magic where every night she feasted, sang and danced. Copying the verses carefully, then binding the clean pages in a leather folio, Cam wrapped it in paper and sent it to Paris.

But the story unfolding beneath his pen now was not for a young girl.

> *By day the maid imprisoned waited,*
> *Persephone's fate she bore,*
> *Till night fell dark and starlight gleamed*
> *Upon the silvery door.*

> *Twelve nights she dwelt among the fey,*
> *Her pleasures richly fed;*

Then brought her, they, a prince of gold
To rest upon her bed.

The maid of stone-bound virtue pure
Drew him upon her cot.
"Sun Prince," she said, "teach me to love
As mortal maid must not."

His pen slowed as the Princess of Sensaire's prose rolled through his thoughts.

When I allow him into my bedchamber, I am beautiful. It is as though his beauty is so expansive it flows from him without effort and I drink it in and it becomes me.

Pure nonsense, of course. The princess was hopelessly naïve. A man did not make a woman beautiful; he could only make her happy. Or not. Case in point: his mother, whose beauty of face and heart had had nothing to do with her husband, but whose spirit had broken further with each cruelty he had visited upon her.

But the princess's fantastical notions of borrowed beauty suited his poem's purpose quite nicely. So too did her curiously not-so-naïve excursions into realms with which he had not imagined a girl of her rank and modesty would be familiar.

Tonight he kissed me.

Much to his interest, she had taken her time getting him to this point. Not holding him off nor inviting more, for pages she'd been content to allow him to touch her.

Or, perhaps, not merely content.

I am waking up. I am alive for the first time in my life. With each caress upon my face, he brings me to life and I feel odd stirrings, sharp stirrings, delicious and forbidden. Then he caresses my hand. He brings our fingers together, palm to palm. His strength is evident but his touch is gentle.

It did not, however, remain gentle. Much as Cam would actually pursue a seduction, with each paragraph she had allowed him to take a bit more liberty upon her—the tender underside of her arm, his hand resting upon her hip then her waist, then both hands, then his fingers threading through her hair, then the pad of his thumb stroking across her lower lip. But each touch, each caress, was at her direct command. In her pages, he did nothing that she did not ask for. By the time she bade him kiss her lips, her prose was drunk on the pleasure of anticipation she herself had created.

The princess knew how to seduce herself, that was clear. The wonder of it was that by the time he'd finished reading the entry and hid the diary away in its spot on the bookshelf, he'd been half-aroused himself.

Must be the novelty of it.

He dipped his pen into the inkpot and set it to the page before him.

> *Of golden eye and reckless joy,*
> *To mortal maid he gave kisses*
> ~~*Soft as down*~~

No. Trite simile.

> *Soft as . . .*
> *Soft as summer ~~moonlight~~ upon swan-white brow.*

Slightly better.

> *Caresses powerful as the ~~tide~~*

Sea? No.

> *Caresses . . . Caresses . . .*

He'd come back to that.

> *Lute, pipe and song filled Paradise,*
> *Night offered up its treasure,*
> *As prince and maid sought full delight*
> *In love's unguarded pleasure.*

Then, like a cinder girl-turned-beauty, the stone princess was changed.

> *The Sun Prince, crowned with magic he,*
> *In love he made her fair,*
> *Till grace of eye and limb were hers,*
> *And lips beyond compare.*

> *With caresses wrought of sun and fire*
> *All powerful as the sea,*

He fashioned her in faery gold
And moonlight just as he.

Dawn came; aroused, the princess wept
To return to mortal's place.
For rich her awakening had been,
And potent love's embrace.

Into the stone-bound world she went.
There her beauty faded,
By ashen dawn's grey pallor swept,
The golden magicks wasted.

When Cam finally drew his pen away he discovered daylight at the windows of his study.

"My lord." His personal man met him with a bow as he entered his bedchamber. "Should you like breakfast brought up?"

"No, Simms. I'll sleep first then take lunch at the club." After that, he would pay a call on his great aunt and make the acquaintance of his intended. With energy rushing through him now, he could face much worse than a coerced betrothal that would win him the only thing he had ever wanted.

He drew off his shirt and donned the dressing gown his valet provided. "By the by, Simms . . ."

"My lord?"

"Have you written your Christmas wish list yet?"

"I have, my lord."

"Would you . . ." This was foolishness. What was he doing?

"My lord?"

"Would you prefer it if I chose a gift for you this year without recourse to that list?"

"I should like that very much, my lord."

Cam blinked. It must be a trick of the light. Simms never grinned.

"All right. Now be off with you. I'm falling asleep on my feet."

His valet departed and he slept.

Later, riding a bit blindly away from his great-aunt's house, Cam was obliged to reconsider his optimism.

Lady Amelia was a diamond of the first water and just as cold. Her silvery-blond curls framed a face of perfect proportions and pale blue eyes well accustomed to appreciation. Her figure was graceful, her dress elegant, and her manner thinly condescending. She expressed her stylishly reserved appreciation of the aspect, arches, roofs, buttresses, windows, terraces, drive, stables, gardens, park and interior appointments of Aylesley as though the estate were hers already. She offered her cool hand to him in parting and her porcelain face did not stir when he slid his thumb across the smooth skin of her palm.

"Good day, my lord," she said without the slightest hint of warmth or embarrassment and drew her hand away.

He didn't know what Lady Amelia knew of him. He didn't particularly care. This was a mercenary arrangement. Both of them would get what they wished from it.

Perhaps he ought to look on the bright side of the coin.

Aylesley was large enough for them to avoid meeting too often. And when even that became intolerable there would always his house in town or Crofton to escape to for relief.

The Marchioness of Dade's dimpled cheeks flickered across his thoughts. She was no longer available, of course. But Lady Cutler-Price, a rounded guinea-bright beauty whose husband preferred the company of a bottle to his wife, had given Cam a clear invitation no more than a sennight ago. He could pay her a call now and lift both their spirits immeasurably. Or he could await nightfall and take his discontent to the tables. When he was out of sorts he always won.

Apparently he had a lifetime of victory at cards to look forward to.

But none of that appealed to him at present. His head ached from lack of sleep and his ink-stained fingers were sore upon the reins. Tucking them into Saladin's golden-white mane, without much thought he guided the stallion across a street and looked up to find himself in front of Reiner's house.

Yes. This would do. Equine minds were remarkable; Saladin, the clever fellow, had brought him to precisely the place he most wished to be. He would have a drink with his friend, then, if he were fortunate, spend a few moments in the library with the diary.

"His royal highness is not in, my lord," the butler said with the muted lisp of his countrymen. Reiner had spent so much time abroad, his English was nearly as clear as Cam's. The princess's accent was more pronounced, particularly soft around the vowels, as though she savored speaking them. "Her majesty is accepting callers," the butler offered.

Where the queen was, her daughter would also be.

Cam regretted it the moment he entered. The princess was not in fact among the dozen ladies and smattering of sycophantic gentlemen clustered about the drawing room. Not entirely bereft of manners, and more importantly not wishing to be ejected by the queen from the royal household on future occasions, he made conversation for a quarter hour while two ladies he knew vaguely fluttered their lashes at him and the queen cast him suspicious glances. When he had endured all he could, he made his escape.

Escape.

He understood the princess now. With Reiner's regular companionship, she could not be entirely unhappy; they were close despite the decade between them in age. But in London her brother mustn't be at home often. Cam would feel the need to escape every night if he were trapped in a house with the Queen of Sensaire every day too.

In the foyer he glanced up the stairwell. A servant lingered on the landing above, busy at some cleaning project. The prospect of sneaking up to the library in the prince and princess's absence did not sit well with him.

The butler proffered his greatcoat.

"Do tell me, good fellow," Cam said in his most insouciant drawl. "Where might I find her royal highness this afternoon?"

"She has gone Christmas shopping, my lord."

"Ah, Christmas shopping," he said casually and wasn't at all certain why he should feel it was hugely important that he speak casually. With the princess he felt casual, after all. A bit guilty for using her diary as his Muse. But casual, nevertheless. "With her brother?"

"With her grace, the Duchess of Lycombe," the butler supplied.

"Excellent," he murmured. His heart beat oddly, with a stuttering sort of jerk-and-halt cadence. He directed Saladin toward Bond Street. The prospect of spending time with his cousin's wife without his cousin hovering protectively by cheered Cam enormously. But when he came upon the pair of ladies laden with packages, followed by a liveried footman equally laden, it was not Arabella's greeting he sought first.

When Princess Jacqueline looked up at him, her pale cheeks were already bright from the chill day. That he felt the need to know if she was still inclined to blush when she encountered him was a troubling notion he thrust aside for consideration later. Or never.

"My lord." Her smile was wide and genuine. It rendered the planes of her face more pleasing even than her impenitent grin. "Have you come Christmas shopping too? Did you remember your valet's list?" A twinkle lit her eyes.

"Upon my oath, with your chastisement in mind I have burned the thing and am now all at a loss," he said. "I have sought you out to beg your assistance in choosing his gift."

Black lashes spread in pleasure. "I did not wish to chastise you, my lord, but to understand."

He waved a hand. "Six of one . . ." He bowed from the saddle to the princess's companion. "Your grace."

Ever skeptical of him, Arabella lifted a cinnamon brow. "Do come down here, my lord, and make yourself useful." She held forth her packages.

He dismounted. "Haven't you servants for this sort of

thing?" He cast a sympathetic glance at the footman. The fellow shrugged. "More servants, rather," he added.

"Of course we do," the princess said, passing her parcels to him as well. "It's just so much more fun to command your gallant assistance."

Command. As she commanded him in her fantasies.

Their eyes met and the rosy hue in her cheeks seemed not to come from the chill December weather but from within her. Her smile wavered.

"Your pleasure, princess, is my sole wish," he said as though his tongue were not in his control. He had offered similar flirtations to more women than he could count. Yet he'd sworn to himself months ago that *this* woman's infatuation he must depress.

This really wasn't the way to accomplish that.

Her gaze dipped—not coquettishly, rather, in a moment of honest confusion that sent a dull spike of something unpleasant beneath his ribs. Then her intelligent eyes came to his again.

"Would that all gentlemen were so obliging," she said smoothly.

All gentlemen? Or other gentlemen? Or *another* gentleman in particular? The last diary entry he'd read was from September. Had she moved on to fantasizing about some other man?

Good Lord, what was he thinking? He couldn't care less if she had replaced him with another fellow. Better for her, in fact. Better for both of them.

"With such companions," he said easily, but his grip on the parcels unnecessarily tight, "they should be."

"Enough already, the two of you," the duchess said. "You may assist us, my lord, but you mustn't tease. We aren't your normal sort of flirts, as you well know."

"Ah," he said. "But why else do you imagine that above all ladies in town I sought out the two of you in particular today?"

"You did?" the princess said. "You sought out us?"

He had. He shouldn't have admitted it. Why he shouldn't have, he didn't know. He was beginning to doubt he knew the reason for anything he did these days.

Aylesley. Of course. Aylesley and the wretched betrothal and his need to lift his spirits after the morning's dispiriting interview.

He gestured to the shop front before them. "This place sells the most intriguing clocks. What of it, your highness? Shall I give a clock to my valet this Christmas? He's always ten minutes ahead of me anyway. This way he might be twenty and I shall be obliged to dismiss him out of sheer irritation. Ah well. I don't suppose a clock will be the thing after all. Terribly foolish of me to have burned that list, I'm beginning to think." He continued on in this vein until the peculiar prickling of discomfort left him and he was once again what he was entirely accustomed to being: a man enjoying the company of women.

He couldn't know.

Could he?

Of course not. How on earth could he have read her diary? Unless Marguerite had read it, told the queen, who'd then told Reiner, who'd then told him.

Ridiculous.

Jacqueline cast a swift glance at the earl as he traded opinions with Arabella on a shop window display, and her legs got shaky. When he'd spoken of pleasure, her mind had sped to what she had written in her diary two days ago, and her cheeks turned to scalding flame.

She must cease writing. He was a real man with a real heart and—oh, dear heaven—a real body, and he deserved respect. But the more she wrote, the more she greeted each morning with anticipation and the more her mother's chastisements rolled off her like water off goose feathers.

Now he turned to her. "What is your opinion on books as gifts, princess? I ask with the knowledge that you are an avid reader as well as writer."

Her throat clogged.

"Ah," he said, his gaze intent upon her, "you do not recall our conversation at the chateau. Ah well." He affected a hopeless sigh. "My poor excuse at conversation fails to make a mark upon a lady so well read and interesting."

"Interesting?" she couldn't help uttering. "My lord, are you perhaps mistaking me for another?"

He took a half step toward her. "It would be impossible for me to mistake you for another, your highness," he said quite close to her. "It is the quiet ladies, you see, who present the greatest mystery and therefore are the most interesting. Indeed, the most intriguing."

"My lord." The air in her lungs was remarkably short. "You seek to flatter but you fall short of the mark."

"Do I?" he frowned. "But I speak honestly."

"I am not accustomed to such honesty, if honesty it is."

"Why not? Has no gentleman ever before admitted that you intrigue him?"

"No." This hurt, though she didn't know why it should. "For no such gentleman has ever existed."

"He does now." He smiled. It was the oddest thing, that smile, not like his charming grins but sincere, as though he were not in fact teasing her. He offered his arm. "Come now, intriguing lady, and offer your opinion on these bookends." He drew her toward the shop window. "I cannot guess what sort of book my valet would like to read, but every man needs a pair of solid brass bookends. If Simms doesn't use them for books, he might instead quash me over the head with them and be rid of me once and for all."

"Mm," she managed. "You are that difficult a master?"

His warm eyes sparkled. "Only when I haven't the desire to please." He lifted her hand and kissed her gloved fingertips. "Only then, your highness."

CHAPTER FIVE

On the afternoon of her mother's supper party Jacqueline accompanied Arabella and her sister, Ravenna, upon their afternoon calls. There they learned that the Earl of Bedwyr was to be married.

"Married?" Arabella gaped, her usual sangfroid forgotten. "But when did this come about?"

"I don't know." The gossip's brow pinched beneath the feather quivering from her turban. "I was hoping, your grace, that as family you might know."

"I don't know a thing about it. But I have not spoken with Lord Bedwyr in over three days."

Jacqueline had. Her heartbeats sped, but heavily and thickly. Only the day before he had called again on Reiner, but when he found her brother absent he remained to assist in the final hanging of decorations in the drawing room in preparation for tonight's party.

Their English housekeeper had insisted that kissing boughs were exceedingly fashionable. When the earl took up the cluster of mistletoe berries and reached up to nestle it in the greenery, stretching coat and breeches over taut muscles in the process, Jacqueline had fought against the flush of heat that arose in her entire body. Then he'd looked over at her and without even a glimmer in his dark eyes asked if she wished to "try it out" immediately.

She had never been so grateful for her mother's entrance into a room than at that moment. He'd given her a private, playful smile, then—outrageously and true to character—repeated the question to the queen.

In the hour before that, which she had spent with him over red velvet ribbons and gold star decorations, he had said nothing of his impending wedding.

"To whom, I wonder, is my husband's cousin betrothed," Arabella said.

The gossip's feather twitched as she turned her attention to the door. "Her."

Two ladies stood in the opening: a woman of superior fashion who surveyed the assembled callers with keen eyes, and a young lady of sublime elegance. While the young lady was not as beautiful as Arabella, her silvery-gold hair shone like silk and her eyes were like the crystal pools that arose from springs in the mountains of Sensaire. Those eyes assessed the room's occupants much as her mother's did, coming to rest on Arabella, shifting briefly to Jacqueline and Ravenna, then returning to Arabella.

They moved toward them, making clear to their hostess their wish for an introduction.

"Your highness," their hostess said, "may I make you acquainted with Lady Maythorpe and her daughter, Lady Amelia? Dear ladies, this is the Princess of Sensaire."

As though unpleasantly startled, the two ladies turned their heads to Jacqueline and sketched the shallowest curtseys. Then Lady Maythorpe's attention shifted back to Arabella. Lady Amelia's lingered in cool disdain upon Jacqueline before she turned to the duchess as well.

Accustomed to such slights from English ladies who were unimpressed with her plain looks, and many of them never having heard of Reiner's small country, Jacqueline reminded herself not to care and tried not to crumble inside, which was perfectly ridiculous. Of course Lord Bedwyr would wed a lady as beautiful as he was handsome.

But after they departed, she relished Ravenna's laughing review of Lady Maythorpe's overbearing condescension and Lady Amelia's chilly hauteur.

"I cannot believe it," Arabella stated as the carriage came to a halt before Jacqueline's house. "Something isn't right about this."

Jacqueline unwound her tongue. "Don't you think Lady Amelia is a suitable bride for Lord Bedwyr?"

"Certainly she's suitable. She is the daughter of an earl, well bred, and beautiful."

"She's an iceberg," Ravenna said. "She'll make him miserable."

"Precisely," Arabella said. "Which is why I cannot fathom why he offered for her."

"Perhaps he didn't," Ravenna said. "Perhaps it's all a hum."

"They came directly to you, Bella," Jacqueline said in a softer voice than she intended. "And Lady Maythorpe spoke of him by name."

"I don't suppose she would have done that unless she

imagined I knew something of the match. He's not exactly on hopeful mothers' lists of eligible bachelors." She worried her lip between her teeth. "Which has suited him perfectly well until now."

The footman opened the carriage door and Jacqueline moved to descend.

Arabella squeezed her hand perhaps a bit too tightly. "I will ask Luc." She had always known. They'd never spoken of it, but since that first day when the earl arrived at the chateau, Jacqueline knew her friend saw through her pretense of indifference to him.

Now she must learn how to actually feel indifferent to him. She always succeeded when she set her mind to an endeavor. If only it was her mind that she must wrest under control this time.

"What is Tarleton doing here?" Cam stood beside his cousin at the door to the drawing room, glasses of port they'd brought from the dining room in hand. "Don't recall him being a regular at this sort of party."

"Reiner's been spending time with him lately," Luc said. "Must be some business of state."

"Dry-as-bones political type, is he?"

"You would know if you ever took your seat in Lords, Cam."

"Don't even think of lecturing me, Captain."

"I have only just succeeded to the peerage."

"After a decade trying to avoid that fate upon the sea." Cam sipped his wine.

"You have held your title for years, wastrel."

"Sticks and stones, coz." He scanned the room for the Princess of Sensaire. Standing with a small cluster of guests, she was looking at him. He smiled and inclined his head. She did not draw her gaze away and her cheeks did not color. Instead, she held his regard soberly, as though she wished to speak with him but knew that in this place and time she could not.

He wished she would. He wished she would throw off the veneer of quiet, controlled grace she affected in public and be the woman he knew from her diary.

The entry he'd read earlier, while guests were still arriving at the queen's party and his brief absence had not been missed, clung to him now. It was a good thing he'd been early; it had taken him a quarter hour of mentally cataloguing the non-existent charms of Lady Amelia Whitley to dampen his arousal. And yet there stood the girl who had made him insensibly hot with only a few vivid paragraphs, wearing pristine white and watching him with clear, candid eyes.

He had never met a woman like her, quietly confident of herself even without the obvious attractions women usually wanted. She was entirely different from the females he was accustomed to knowing and—as the faery prince did to the mortal princess in his poem—she made him feel alive in a strange, new way, as though his other world of license was nothing more than a foggy sleep. He hadn't played cards for weeks, and he'd had no desire lately to find a willing wife and indulge as he liked best. He reminded himself that he would be married within weeks. If he were going to indulge, it must be now or never again.

But he was confused. He knew it to be because of the inspiration her fantasies gave him to write. It certainly wasn't her. She never flirted, never batted her lashes, never accidentally brushed her bosom against his arm, and never touched him unless he took her hand and obliged her to. She did not fawn over him, and he was fascinated by the contrast of the emotion and passion in her diaries and the reticent exterior she showed to the world. It was a remarkable challenge to reconcile the princess by day with the writer by night. Where the princess was demure and reserved, the diary entries were becoming increasingly torrid. That he was the only one that knew of the fantasies her imagination conjured made it all the worse.

It drove him a little wild

She simply could not be the author. No woman was that proficient at dissembling. He was expert enough in the breed to trust his judgment on this.

With that in mind, he bid his cousin adieu and made his way around the chamber to her. As if she knew his intention, she drew away from her companions and came toward him, but not circuitously as he did. Instead she came directly.

"Your highness," he said below the burble of conversations. "You have just snubbed the Baroness of Crawford."

"Have I?" Her fine eyes were alight and her mouth offered him the smile he found himself wishing she reserved for him alone. "I must be terribly rude."

"On her afternoon calls tomorrow she will undoubtedly inform her every acquaintance of your outrageous foreign snobbery."

"She did not notice I passed. None of them ever do."

"Why—"

"Oh, let's not talk about that," she said hurriedly. "Tell me what you wished to speak with me about."

"Did I?"

"Of course you did. You were staring at me from all the way across the room." Her tongue was sweet and gentle over the harsh Saxon syllables of his native language. She wrote in French, the language most of her people adopted at birth—though Cam had learned from her diary that the Sensaire dialect was, in some instances, quite a different thing indeed. He wished he knew the endearments she spoke to her fantasy version of him.

"I thought it rather the opposite," he said honestly.

"Oh, it could not have been, my lord. Princesses do not stare."

He glanced aside. "Only queens, I suppose."

She shifted her attention to her mother and released a short breath of frustration.

"Daggers, as they say," he murmured.

"Daggers indeed."

"She doesn't like it when I speak with you, does she?" he said because he knew it to be true, and justifiably so. If Claire were eight years older, he wouldn't like her talking to a man like him either.

"No. She does not. But I do." She seemed to study him. Her lips parted, then closed abruptly.

"Your highness?" he said quietly.

"Sometimes," she said upon a rush of air, "I wish that I were an entirely different person and not a princess at all."

He watched her eyes, wide and without any hint of spoiled complaint in them. "Do you?"

"Yes. For instance, I wish that I were standing here wearing a shockingly red satin gown and singing Christmas carols at the top of my lungs."

He chuckled. "Do you like singing, princess?"

"*Singing?*" Twin creases appeared between her brows. "What about the red gown? Shouldn't you ask me about that first?"

"Probably. But since I should like to see you wearing a shockingly red satin gown, it wasn't my principal curiosity."

Her mouth split into a perfect smile.

"Now you've done it," he said. "Your mother will have you cleaning the floors in punishment for that grin."

Candlelight twinkled in her eyes. "Princesses do not grin, my lord."

"Perhaps not. But they smile beautifully."

The beautiful smile disappeared.

Cam's chest got peculiarly tight. "What have I said?"

She dropped her gaze. "I must go. Maman expects me to speak with all of our guests tonight—"

"Except me."

"—and I haven't yet." She gave him an elegant nod and left him standing alone, bemused and wondering how he had hurt her, or if indeed he had, and more importantly what he might do to make up for it.

But now he knew for certain that she was the author of the diary. Of course she was. He was a fool to have ever doubted it, albeit a fool with a precious secret much more shocking than a red satin gown.

A Prussian general.

A Portuguese prince.

An English duke.

These were her choices, Reiner told her. As she stood at the top of the steps of the ballroom of one of society's most fashionable hostesses upon her brother's arm, she promised him she would accept whichever he chose for her. Then she looked across the crowds of people and saw the Earl of Bedwyr, and all the hard work she had accomplished in the fortnight since her mother's supper party seemed entirely for naught.

He had called upon them many times in the intervening days, always to see Reiner then spending more time with her than her brother. One morning he had taken her and Arabella up in his carriage for a ride in the park, then when rain drove them inside he treated them to tea at an elegant hotel instead. Another day he walked with her in the neighborhood. And on yet another day he'd gone Christmas shopping with them again.

He was a kind, amusing companion, generous with sharing his enjoyment of life, interested in art, books, and of course poetry, and as little conceited as she had imagined him months earlier. He seemed not to notice when ladies who passed them fluttered their lashes at him, nor when shopkeepers flirted with him, nor when women dropped their kerchiefs before him. He simply picked them up, proffered them with an elegant bow, then continued along as before.

Jacqueline had trained herself to ignore his flatteries, which she knew to be untruths and certainly uttered to all women out of habit. But she did not succeed in resisting her unwise feelings. She was no longer infatuated with him. No emotion so superficial could explain the ache in her chest now when she met his gaze from across the room and, with a quick nod to his companions, he started toward her.

"Your highness." He bowed low over her hand and his warm smile seemed all for her.

"Good of you to say hello, Bedwyr," her brother remarked dryly.

"Hello," he said perfunctorily, his eyes sparkling at Jacqueline. "Do you dance tonight, princess?"

"Not with you," Reiner said, perusing the crowd.

The earl followed his attention. "Looking for someone?"

"Tarleton. Have you seen him?"

"No, but I've not been searching for him." He leaned toward her. "No red gown tonight, princess?" he whispered beneath the rising music.

"Not yet," she whispered in reply. "But I have grand plans."

"Excellent." He had not blinked an eye at Reiner's refusal to allow her to dance with him.

Not three yards away, a tiny lady of advanced years and draped in snug-fitting black caught his attention with a quick snap of her wrist.

"Is that Lady Rowdon?" Reiner said.

"Great-auntie? Yes." He cast Jacqueline a tolerantly amused glance. "Duty calls. I wish you both a diverting evening." He bowed and headed toward Lady Rowdon. As he neared, Lady Maythorpe moved to Lady Rowdon's side, her perfect daughter in tow. The earl gave her a bow that Jacqueline was pleased to see was not nearly as deep as the bow he had given to her. Then he extended his arm and led Lady Amelia in to the set that was forming.

Jacqueline's pleasure disintegrated. No betrothal announcement had been made, but matters seemed clear enough.

"Jackie?"

She turned from the tableau of the gorgeous couple to her brother's sober face.

"The general is not attending this ball tonight," he said. "If you wish, we can leave."

"I thought you preferred the Duke of Tarleton."

"I prefer your happiness. If that happiness will be better secured far from England . . ." He glanced toward his friend dancing with Lady Amelia. "Then I will be content."

She wanted to throw her arms around him and tell him that he was the best of all brothers. Instead she set her shoulders. "No. Let us search out the duke now. Then, if I am very good perhaps you will allow me to dance with him, do you think?"

A dent creased his cheek. "I think I will allow that."

"A princess should have at least one dance at a ball." Even if her brother must arrange it for her, and even if it was not with the man she wanted who would never be hers.

As the pale English sun was just beginning to peek through the treetops, Jacqueline was putting her mare through its paces in the park, her groom following, when on the rise appeared a golden god upon a magnificent white steed. The cold air swirled about the great beast's distended nostrils and—as though the hands that guided it were uncertain—the animal pawed the ground.

Then Lord Bedwyr spurred his mount down the hill toward her and came to her side.

"Good morning, princess. I am astonished to see you abroad at such an hour. Didn't you dance holes through your slippers last night?"

"But you are here as well. I could ask the same of you."

"I don't wear slippers, of course." He leaned in and whispered, "Not nearly manly enough."

"Do gentlemen ever wear away the soles of their shoes dancing?"

"I don't know. Perhaps we should ask my valet. He knows everything."

"He does not know what you are giving him for Christmas this year."

"He does not, in fact. Thanks to you."

"What did you choose?"

"A position for his wife in my household." He watched her now quite carefully it seemed. "It is a surprise he will not anticipate."

Jacqueline's throat was tight. A bachelor for years, with a wife upon the horizon he must now be preparing to expand his household.

"That is very good of you, my lord."

"Not good. I am never good, princess." His brow was drawn, a tousled lock of hair shading serious dark eyes. Then he shifted his gaze ahead and seemed to study the trees from which cold mists arose before them.

"How is Lady Amelia?" Her words were unplanned, but she was glad she said them. He may as well know she knew.

He turned to her sharply. "What?"

"Rather, who. Lady Amelia Whitley. Your betrothed."

"Not quite yet," he said. "How is it you come by this premature information?"

"Everybody knows." She shrugged and his gaze slipped to her shoulder then back to her face.

"Everybody knows what, exactly?"

"That Lady Rowdon is keen for you to wed Lady Amelia. Why?"

His perfect mouth curved upward. "Princess, have I told you how greatly I admire your forthrightness?"

"I don't see why you should. Maman condemns me for it daily."

"My great-aunt has long disapproved of my style of living and wishes to see me leg shackled before she gives up the ghost."

"That was baldly said."

He scratched the back of his neck and nodded. "And not the entire truth."

"What is the entire truth?"

"I fear I am not at liberty to say at this time."

"I don't suppose you will ever be at liberty to say, will you?"

"Probably not. But, my dear, this is a dreadfully dull topic, don't you agree? Tell me, instead, what have you been reading of late? Have you allowed the frippery fashions of London society to influence you? Do you now fill your hours with cheap comedies and gothic horrors, obliging me to admit myself sorely disappointed in your good sense?"

So this is how it would be, and she must be content with it. She could not be in love with him; she could never allow herself to be so foolish. In her diary she gave him both her heart and her body, but in reality she must never give him either. "Oh, I am far too sensible for gothic novels," she said with what she hoped appeared a laughing eye. "And lately," she added more honestly, "I haven't the temperament for comedies."

He turned that seeking gaze upon her that she had seen before, as though he wished to see into her thoughts and to know what she did not say aloud. Her breaths came shallowly. Here, upon this path, she could melt into his eyes and be content forever. But friends did not melt into each other's eyes while riding through the park.

"I daresay you don't," he only said.

Unhappiness twined inside her. "I think I may not like it that you said that."

"I don't believe low comedy suits you," he replied quite seriously. "You are too—"

"Humorless?"

He lifted a brow. "I shan't admit what I intended to say."

"Why not?"

"Because you would slap my face, then we would part as bitter acquaintances rather than good friends. I much prefer the latter."

"Then you mustn't tell me, indeed." And she would not tell him her thoughts. At least that way they would remain equals in their friendship.

He assisted her to dismount before her house, holding her for the briefest instant before his grip loosened. She looked up, and his hands once again tightened around her waist. In his warm eyes was something very strange. A question, or perhaps a doubt.

"I . . . I . . ." he twice began. "I will step inside and see if I can find your brother at home," he finished and finally released her, but he did not step back.

"It is barely nine o'clock," she said a little breathlessly, to her thorough shame. "You are likely to find him still abed."

Above his cravat, his throat jerked in a thick swallow. "I daresay I might," he said and gestured her inside.

The butler informed them that his highness was in the breakfast parlor.

"Ah, I am in luck," the earl said, but his gaze was oddly bright. With a crooked grin, he lifted her hand and raised it to his lips, turning the tingles in her belly into fireworks. "Good day, princess." He went swiftly up the stairs.

She curled her fingertips into her palm and walked to her brother's study. Reiner's secretary had prepared a dossier on the Duke of Tarleton and her brother wished her to read it before she made her final decision. No other brother would be so generous. She was beyond fortunate.

"Maman?" she said upon entering the study. "And Reiner? I thought you were at breakfast."

"I've just finished. Have you come for this?" He proffered a stack of pages.

"I have."

Her brother and mother exchanged glances.

"I know my duty," Jacqueline said firmly. "Your concern is unmerited."

Her brother's eyes were troubled.

"When the New Year comes, we will expect your compliance, Jacqueline," the queen said.

"You will have it," she said docilely, but caged anger stirred in her. She knew her duty, yes. She had even cordoned off her heart to make fulfilling her duty easier. But perhaps that had merely been a lie she'd told herself to guard against greater hurt even than marrying where she did not wish. Perhaps if she continued to lie, her heart would someday believe it. But she doubted it.

"Lord Bedwyr accompanied me back from the park," she said, a hint of defiance in her voice, and turned her attention sharply from her mother to her brother. "Bowdon informed him that you were in the breakfast parlor."

Reiner stood up. "Half the time I think Bedwyr doesn't come here to see me." He paused at the door. "I daresay our chef's excellent preparations draw him."

"I daresay," she said with a shrug. Avoiding her mother's gaze, she settled into a chair with the file on the duke. In her half-dozen encounters with him she'd learned that Duke Tarleton was actively political and a responsible landowner. While not as handsome as Lord Bedwyr—no man on earth was—he was attractive and taller than her by several inches. His conversation was mostly of politics and books, both of which she could appreciate, although not always the political philosophy he preferred.

She had begun to read the dossier on his estates when her brother retuned alone.

"Bedwyr's left already," he said.

"Lord Bedwyr is mercurial," the queen said coolly.

Jacqueline rubbed her thumb over her knuckles that had felt the heat of his lips and could not agree. The Earl of Bedwyr was not Mercury.

He was Apollo.

Cam paced his study, boots and hair still damp from his morning's ride that had been interrupted by the appearance of the Princess of Sensaire.

Dammit, but he should have trusted in his instincts and not gone to meet her when he caught that glimpse of her across the park. Yesterday the diary entry he'd read had flattened him, and he hadn't yet quite recovered.

To his knowledge, he had never before taken a woman's virginity. Now, apparently, he had. At least in fiction.

Moreover, he had enjoyed every moment of it. *In reality.*

After that, at the ball it had been torture to greet her lightly, to look into her lovely eyes and not confess all. He should never have allowed this to continue. From that first day at the chateau he should have forgotten the diary and remained pleasantly aloof with her. He should never have continued reading and, above all, he should have never become friends with her.

But he'd been weak, and somewhat vain, and in need of distraction from the course his actual life was taking. And he liked her. It was as simple as that.

But after the acute discomfort of the ball—where he had been obliged to partner his great-aunt's choice when he wished instead to be dancing with his not-so-innocent friend, to be discovering whether holding her in reality was as shattering as it was in the pages of her diary—after that he had vowed to himself that he would no longer seek out her company. Not under any circumstances. Then in the park, with a sleepless night muddling his head, he should have turned around, finished Saladin's exercise, and gone about his business for the remainder of the day, blissfully unaware of what he knew now.

She knew about Lady Amelia. Apparently everyone knew. Friends at the ball had confirmed that. Not liking his hesitation, Lady Rowdon had spread the gossip to try to force his hand.

But that was not what now had him digging his heels into the thick rug on the floor of his study and raking his hands through his hair. Every word of her latest diary entry was emblazoned on his memory like they had been burned there with fire.

He enters the chamber and the candlelight makes his skin golden like his hair as he draws off his dressing gown. I am on my bed, on my stomach with my head turned aside on the pillow, watching him approach. The mattress is soft beneath my thighs; the tips of my breasts brushing the bed linen are taut in anticipation.

Then he is behind me. I stare out the window at the moon that bathes me in light.

He removes his clothing but leaves mine, only drawing the skirt up my calves and thighs, and I sigh at the caress of silk slipping along my skin. He does not touch me. He bares my buttocks. The chamber is cold, but he is near and I am lit from within. When he finally touches me, the slightest caress on the insides of my knees, that fire within heats me so that I do his bidding. My thighs part, my toes curl under.

I know what he will bid me do next. As though I dream I feel his hands, certain and so strong, around my hips. He lifts them and I offer no resistance. I have, after all, asked him for this. I have demanded it.

Cam tugged at the cravat squeezing his throat, but he still couldn't breathe.

The trouble was not in his lungs.

Aside from no little frustration over the raging erection that had been straining the fall of his breeches since he'd read the passage, any number of questions galloped through his head. Why didn't she want him to remove her nightrail? Why did neither of them speak? Why wasn't the fire built up and the chamber warm? And most importantly, how in the hell did she know what he would bid her do next and from what scoundrel had she learned it?

But all his questions paled beneath the vibrant colors in his imagination as he fantasized taking her from behind in her bed, his hands clasping her creamy buttocks, his cock straining to thrust deeper, to give her pleasure as he took it.

Did she become aroused when she wrote in her diary? As aroused as he became reading it? She *must*. Did she touch herself? Did she come dreaming that he was making her come— his hands, his tongue, his hungry cock inside her? Or did she know nothing of real pleasure yet? Did she only suspect it? Did she lie alone in her bed at night, her lips parted, breaths quick and shallow, her body throbbing helplessly, without hope of satisfaction as her imagination painted portraits of him pleasuring her?

He wanted to pleasure her. In all ways. He wanted to make her smile and laugh and cry out in blind ecstasy. He wanted to actually take her virginity, to give her the greatest gift he knew and to watch her face as she discovered the miracle that he'd long since taken for granted. He wanted to be her first, the god she imagined him to be.

But it wasn't only that, he knew in the pit inside him. With her—inexperienced, clever, too smart for him, and far too honest—he wanted to be a good man. He wanted to be a better man. He wanted to deserve the friendship she was offering him. That in another reality, another world, she might offer him her body as well could remain a tantalizing dream. But in this reality, he wanted—needed—to give her more than pleasure. He needed to give her comfort.

"It's what you do," the marchioness had said one morning before dawn when he was dressing.

"What do I do, sweeting?" he had replied as he drew on his boots.

"You comfort unhappy women," she said sleepily. "Me, and your mistresses before me. Desperately unhappy women trapped in horrid marriages." She sighed upon a smile. "Cam Westfall, Lord of Comfort."

He had sat stunned for a moment, but he'd held onto his temper until he was outside. Then he'd ridden Saladin through the park as fast as the stallion would go, working the anger from his muscles.

The princess was unhappy; that much had been clear to him from the first day at the chateau. Later he had come to appreciate her sweetness of temper and strength of character, but those had not masked the sadness in her eyes. To be so reserved on the exterior yet so passionate within must tear her apart. So he'd done it again, Lord of Comfort attempting to accomplish the impossible.

But the circumstances were not typical. She was not an unhappily married woman and he was most certainly not a god. And the long and the short of it was that he simply wanted to take her to bed for a good, hot satisfying fuck that would render her fantasies tame in comparison.

He stood in the middle of his study, both hands sunk in his hair, and groaned long and loud. He covered his eyes with his palms.

No. No no no.

She was his Muse, for God's sake. He could not degrade her so. His cock was an unbridled beast, but he was a man of at least some remnants of honor. He would tamp down this need and maintain her honor and what existed of his.

Throwing his ruined cravat aside, he marched up to his bedchamber where Simms provided a newly starched linen and clean boots. Then he mounted his horse and went to his cousin's house. He would tell Luc about Aylesley and Lady Rowdon's plan and seek advice. His cousin was an irritatingly proud son of a bitch, but he was a clever one.

He only realized his true motive for calling upon his cousin when he learned that the princess was not with the duchess as she often was mornings, seeking to escape her mother's yoke for a few precious hours. All potential pleasure in the day fled.

He was an idiot.

"Cam?" Luc stood at the top of the stairs. "Why are you standing there staring at the door?" He started down the steps. "You look wretched."

"Thanks, coz. I feel splendid. By the by, that scar across your face is dreadfully red lately. Might want to consider a larger piece of fabric to conceal it. Or perhaps a bag to cover the entire head."

Luc leveled an implacable stare. "I assume you have come here with a purpose?"

"I may be reconsidering that."

"Like you reconsidered the ball last night? When Arabella went looking for you before supper, you'd already left."

"I had." He hadn't been able to bear another moment of it. "But how delightful to be searched for by a beauty. What did your lovely wife need of me, I wonder?"

"Reiner told her that he and the queen have fixed on a short list of candidates for Princess Jacqueline's hand."

A hard ball of something that felt suspiciously like lead lodged in Cam's stomach. "Is that so?" he drawled. "And your duchess wished to share this information with me because . . . ?"

"Jacqueline won't tell Arabella about her preferences in the matter. My wife wishes to learn what you know."

"How should I know anything?"

"It's no secret that you've been in the princess's company frequently over the past several weeks. Reiner said you've given her some relief from the queen's company and sought to make her more comfortable in society."

"It was my pleasure." His voice didn't sound like him.

"That was your intention," Luc said slowly. "Wasn't it? To help her feel more comfortable in London?"

"Yes." *He had to know who was on that list.* "Of course." He turned toward the door. "Now I must be off. Appointment I'd forgotten, don't you know."

"No, I don't know."

"Spoil sport."

"Cam—"

"Lucien." He looked over his shoulder. "If you pester me along these lines you will get nothing from it but the point of my sword across your other eye—"

"I dare you to try it."

"And as I have already taken the one, I should be bored with the repetition. Good day, coz."

Mounting Saladin, he flirted with the idea of finding Tony and getting rip roaring drunk. The naval captain could always be depended upon to have a batch of it, and Cam had barely seen him in weeks. But he feared that no good could come from further encounters with his friends or even strangers today. And he could not—*would not*—return to Reiner's house and demand to see that list.

So he went home and, finally, to sleep.

CHAPTER SIX

Cam awoke to the dark hours of the morning, read by the light of a candle until day broke, then took Saladin to the park.

The princess was not there. He had half-hoped and half-dreaded she would be. But this morning she did not oblige, and he returned to his house and a breakfast he could not eat. He could not recall the last time he'd eaten. Before reading her diary two days ago, perhaps?

He stared in dismay at his meal growing cold before him and again considered his liquor cabinet. Then he considered paying a call on the decidedly non-virginal Lady Cutler-Price. Instead he went into his study and wrote two stanzas. When he finished, he cast them into the fire. Then he played a game of chess against himself. After that he wrote two more stanzas and watched them burn too. Restlessness lapped at him relentlessly.

The post arrived. He discarded most of the invitations and another note from Lady Cutler-Price, set the *Times* aside for later, and perused the latest report from his steward at

Crofton. It was modestly hopeful news. He penned a quick letter in response.

Then he sat and stared out the window.

When the clock struck two, he changed his cravat and coat, called for Saladin to be saddled, and rode to Reiner's house.

The prince was not in, the butler told him. Nor was the queen. They had gone to Richmond for the day.

Was her highness perhaps receiving?

Within moments he was being announced at the parlor door. She sat at the pianoforte plucking out a dull tune with one finger. When the butler spoke his name, her face lit in pleasure.

"Good day, my lord. What brings you here today?"

He made a show of glancing curiously about the chamber. "Empty, your highness? In the absence of your brother and the queen, is your butler instructed to turn away all rogues and scoundrels except me?"

"Oh, no," she said with a light wave of her hand. "All the other rogues and scoundrels have made appointments for later. You are simply early."

"Really?"

"No. Of course not. You may arrive at any hour you wish. Within reason, of course." She gave him the little smile he had come to understand meant she was pleased with him, with herself, and with their conversation—the smile that told him she was, for the moment, happy.

"I meant about your appointments with other rogues and scoundrels," he clarified.

"Oh." She turned on the bench to face him. "No to that

too. No rogues to speak of lately. Except you, of course." As always, she wore a white gown of exquisite fabric and simple design, and her hair was pulled away from her face in the style she'd once said her mother preferred for her. He wondered what style she preferred. Her diary never specified. He wanted to ask her.

"That isn't what I have heard," he said as the footman closed the door.

"It isn't?" Her brow rose. "Are stories being bandied about of rogues and scoundrels beating down our door? *Sacre bleu*."

He allowed himself a slight smile, but urgency drove his persistence. "Rather, your brother mentioned a list of scoundrels—rather, suitors—that are welcome in this house of late."

Her eyes shuttered. "They are not scoundrels."

"No?" He took a step forward and she stood abruptly. He paused. A moment stretched during which neither of them spoke or moved.

Then she went around the instrument to the window. "They are the three gentlemen that Reiner and my mother have determined would be the most suitable husband for me."

Who? "Husband?"

She glanced over her shoulder. "I am to wed just after the New Year. Didn't you know?"

No. And why neither Reiner, Luc nor Arabella had mentioned it to him he did not wish to ponder. "I might have heard something to that effect." He propped his hip against the back of a chair in a pose of sublime nonchalance. "I understand young ladies look forward to such things with glee. You must be thrilled."

"And yet I am not. I suppose I am very contrary."

"Ah." He could say nothing else.

"It isn't the wedding that displeases me, or having my husband chosen for me. I have known forever that my marriage must be a matter of state," she explained in perfectly neutral terms while Cam's pulse raced.

"Then you are not in need of commiseration?" he said.

Her brows shot high. "Did you imagine that I was?"

He shrugged, his tongue somewhat thick.

"Did you think I was as unhappy about my imminent wedding as you are about yours, and you came to comfort me in my distress?" she asked. "How kind you are, my lord."

"I didn't—"

"Don't try to deny that you are displeased with Lady Rowdon's plans. I may not have a wide acquaintance of gossips in London, but I am not entirely naïve, you know."

Much less naïve than most women of his acquaintance, it seemed. "I would never suggest such a thing."

"At least you won't be at a significant disadvantage when you wed," she said thoughtfully.

"Disadvantage?"

"There is . . ." Her voice trailed off. She looked out the window and tilted her head. Her stance was relaxed. This conversation did not, apparently, agitate her as it did him.

"Princess?"

"The thing is, I have never kissed a man," she said and looked over her shoulder at him. "Will my husband be disappointed to discover that I have no knowledge of kissing?"

Cam's throat had gone entirely dry. If she had no actual knowledge of kissing, she certainly had excellent intuition.

"Why do you ask me?"

"I cannot very well ask Reiner. How horridly embarrassing that should be." She scowled but her eyes twinkled.

"You might ask your ladies in waiting, or the Duchess of Lycombe."

"How would they know the answer? They are women."

He was nonplused. "Well . . ."

She turned to him fully. "You and I are friends, so I trust you will answer me honestly. I know you have considerable experience kissing women."

His cravat had shrunk again. "Do you?"

She lifted a single, eloquent brow. She was far too intelligent for him, and far too forthright, and he was far too accustomed to consorting with females of much less acute minds and much baser characters. She was not now flirting with him but making a statement of fact.

He nodded in silent admission.

Both brows perked now, like the shimmering feathers of a raven. "So . . .?"

"I should think that your husband would be delighted to teach you the finer points of kissing." And learn a thing or two in the process.

"I suppose you may be correct about that. Men like to instruct women. I think it makes them feel more in control."

He could not hide his amusement. "You don't say?"

"Well, doesn't it? You are a man."

"Good of you to notice."

"Do you like it when you feel in control of a woman?"

"I like it when a woman feels she is getting what she wants from me."

Her fine, expressive eyes widened. Then, slowly, she turned to the pianoforte and began rearranging the music on the stand. Cam studied the clean sweep of her back to her gently curved hips and the straight set of her shoulders. She was not petite, not enticingly round, not anything he had ever desired in a woman. But merely looking at her back and knowing what she imagined of him—*of them together*—made his heartbeats hard.

"I should like to give it a try before I marry," she said without turning around. Her voice was pitched a bit low. "Kissing, that is." She glanced at him. Her cheeks were ever so slightly pink.

"Should you?" He suspected where this was going. He'd been the object of countless women's flirtations. But never this woman. She confined her attentions to him safely in her diary.

This was a different woman before him now.

"Yes," she said. "I think it would be a useful experience to take into marriage. Don't you?" She turned her hungry gaze upon him and Cam's entire body flooded with heat.

He tried to ignore it. *She was his Muse.* She was inspiration and clarity in his life of restless discontent. She was not an object of desire.

He wished his body understood that.

He should not have come.

"Perhaps." He ran his hand around the back of his neck and tried to breathe evenly. This would be a good moment to take his leave.

She set down the final sheets of music and closed the lid. "I would need a willing gentleman, of course. One unafraid that I would seek to entrap him. A gentleman who knows me well and I could trust not to tell anyone else, and upon whom I haven't the slightest designs."

"That would undoubtedly be wise." He should leave. He should go to the door and through it and out of the house. With great speed. "Are you acquainted with such a man?" He. Must. Leave. *Now*.

"I don't know." Her lips screwed into a twist and she seemed to pause in her willful rush toward indiscretion. "Am I?"

Cam didn't like it that she asked. He didn't like it that she did not trust him entirely to be her friend. He didn't like what that said about her opinion of his character. That he was thoroughly guilty of her mistrust, including his intentions toward her at the present moment, was a hypocrisy he was glad to delay contemplating for another time.

"I believe there is such a man in this very parlor, your highness." He should cut out his tongue. It was the only solution. He couldn't very well cut off the other part of him that was rebelling from his best intentions. It was his favorite appendage.

Her black lashes made several swift beats. "You would do it? Without worrying that I would tell my brother or mother or Arabella or anybody? And without telling anyone yourself?"

"Come now. We are friends enough that I believe you know you can trust me." Trust him to know her most fervent dreams and fantasies and not tell a soul including her? Yes, she could trust him. He was a villain. "Shall I teach you how to kiss your husband, princess?"

"I don't know." She hesitated. "Will I like it?"

He deserved that. "I suspect so."

"But will I like it enough to want to do it with my husband? Otherwise there will be no point to it. And if I do not like it, it could potentially have negative consequences."

He deserved every single word that thrust daggers into his taut groin and overinflated egoism now. Her forthright manner and good heart made him believe she did not intend the abuse. But the wanton fantasies recorded in the pages of her diary made him seriously doubt that.

"You will like it." He walked toward her. "If your husband truly cares for you, you will like everything about your wifely duties to him."

"Wifely duties." She smiled, but the curve of her lower lip quivered. "You sound like my mother."

"Then I should stop talking." He closed the distance between them and took her chin between his fingers. He tilted her face up.

Her eyes were wide and abruptly wary. "I did not intend—"

He caught her open lips and held them so with his. She had a generous mouth; it fit to his perfectly. She tasted sweet, like some subtle combination of fresh herbs and honey. She remained completely still until he drew away.

"Thank you," she said, her quick breaths stealing over his lips. "That was instructive."

"I'm not finished." He allowed his hand to cup her jaw and his fingertips to strafe the edge of her hair. It was silky and thick, as he had imagined. "May I continue?"

"Yes."

This time she was ready, her lips pliant as they met his,

sparking his need to truly teach her how to kiss a man. Tasting her gently, guardedly, holding in check the urgency that grew in him with each touch of her lips and each soft gasp of surprise, Cam gave the Princess of Sensaire her first real kiss.

Long ago he had stopped thinking much about the act of kissing in favor of simply employing it to his lovers' greatest benefit, and his. Now the princess's innocence was his undoing. She sought his mouth as though she were discovering a new land, eagerly yet uncertain, each brush of her untried lips against his asking him to show her the way. Allowing the tip of his tongue to trail along the seam of her mouth, he ever so gently sucked on her lower lip. Upon a sigh of wonderment, her mouth fell open. And Cam finally felt the heat inside her.

He could not halt this with a chaste kiss.

Sinking his fingers into her hair he drew her toward him so that her breasts grazed his chest. With half-lidded eyes and her parted lips damp from his kiss, she looked up at him and said, "More."

He gave her what she wished. What he wished. What he'd wished for weeks, he understood now. Dipping between her lips for an instant, a shallow exploration, he drank in her heat. Then, with every mote of self-control in his body engaged, he made himself retreat.

A little sound of protest arose in her throat.

Invitation enough.

He delved. She gasped, then took him in, allowing him to stroke her tongue and offering a soft moan of acceptance.

Again he made himself break the kiss. His chest rose hard upon thick breaths. "Princess—"

"I was not certain he would do that," she said quickly, her voice husky.

He? Who in the—

"My husband-to-be," she reminded him.

Cam squeezed his eyes shut and held her off him. "Princess—"

"What else might he do?" Her eyes were bright with desire and sheer delirious happiness.

He could not deny her.

"This." He pulled her flush against him. She was ready when he lowered his head and covered her mouth, opening to him and meeting him with fervor. Her body against his was slender, her breasts small, and he wanted his hands on them and all over her. Gripping her waist with one hand, he slid the other to the nape of her neck and slanted his mouth across hers and kissed her as he wished, without regard for her chastity or indeed anything but satisfying the frustrated lust she'd built in him with pages of innocently erotic fantasies.

It did not satisfy. The more he took of her, the more he wanted.

He pulled away and she gulped in air like a fish cast out of water. Silently cursing himself and her both, he loosened his hold on her and began to step back. Her hands came up, her fingers dug into the fabric of his coat sleeves, and she pressed her mouth to his anew.

He needed no further convincing. She was sweetly soft and devastatingly eager, innocence and passion combined. The gentle pressure of her thighs and breasts against him was like brandy in his blood. He smoothed his hand over her back and down, and cupped her buttock.

"He will do that?" Her breaths were strained.

"He might." He would. He wouldn't be able to stop himself from it.

He bent to her mouth anew, caressing her tongue as his hand caressed. Tension vibrated through her stillness, and she gripped his sleeves tighter. The delicate fabric of her gown gave way and his fingers strafed the soft crevice between her thighs. A quiver rippled through her. Hand spread on her behind, he pulled her hips tight against his and a moan caught in her throat where her pulse was a fluttering creature. He placed his mouth over this evidence of her passion, tasted the softness of her skin, and she swallowed a whimper of pleasure.

"Am I supposed to remain immobile and passively accept his caresses?" she said breathlessly. "Is that expected?"

"No." His hands swept up her sides, his thumbs curving beneath her breasts. They were small, firm, and intoxicating beyond belief. There were so many details of her to be learned, a garden of subtle beauty waiting for his exploration. "Positively not."

"What should I do?"

"Touch him." *What was he saying?*

"Touch *him*?"

No. "Yes." He would regret this.

"Where?"

He pulled her slender fingers from his sleeve and covered his erection with her hand and held her there. "Here." His voice was too rough. This should not be happening. He should not be encouraging her and more importantly he should not feel her innocent touch like a brand of fire on his body.

She hiccupped. Then her fingers closed around the fabric of his breeches. He could not contain his shuddering exhale.

"So, this is what it feels like," she said a bit wonderingly.

"That—" He kissed her neck as she squeezed him gently and he saw stars. "Is what it feels like."

Hesitantly, she stroked her hand along the length of him. "Why does touching you here make *me* feel liquid and hot?"

"Because your body wants it."

"I know," she whispered. "At least, I suspected."

She had suspected him into a frenzy several mornings while reading her diary. And now she was putting her suspicions to expert use. Tentatively her hand explored and his cock jerked beneath the caress. He pressed into her palm, needing her to touch him harder. He could not endure another moment of this teasing. He hadn't sufficient self-control. He never had, but he'd never before put himself to the test.

Grasping her hand gently he removed it from him. But he could not tear himself away. Not just yet.

"I can give your body what it wants without assailing your virginity."

"I know that too," she admitted.

He knew she knew it, but he was not certain to what extent. "You know quite a lot for an unmarried girl."

"I read."

"I'd like to borrow your books."

"Do it." She pressed her entire body against him. "Please. I want to feel it. So—so I will know what to expect."

She was lying now, which in his lust-induced haze was sufficient justification for Cam to conclude that she was perfectly fair game.

"Sit down," he said.

"Sit down?"

He took her hand and drew her to a sofa away from the window. That her hand in his like this, palm to palm, her fingertips tucked trustingly against his knuckles, made his heart beat harder than her hand on his cock had, sent warning bells clanging in his head. He ignored them.

"It can be overwhelming," he said, guiding her down onto the sofa and looking into her lovely eyes the color of Kentish rain and wide as a summer storm, unable to release her hand quite yet.

"Oh." Her throat constricted in a little swallow.

A pinpoint of conscience pricked him, not hard enough to release her and get the hell out of this house, but uncomfortable enough to momentarily check his lust. "You needn't do this."

"But I do need to," she said like a woman who knew her mind, slipped her fingers into his hair, and gave him the sweetest, most honestly hungry kiss he had ever received.

"I am going to touch you now." Indeed, he could not stop himself from doing so. "Where he would touch you." He nearly choked on the words.

"Yes, please," she said breathlessly in his ear, the barest brush of her lips like a drug to him. And so he touched her, first on her waist, then her belly, then her breast. She leaned into the caresses, her eyelids fluttering shut and sighed. "I had wondered . . ." she murmured, then caught her breath as he found her nipple beneath layers of fabric. "*Ohh.*"

Then he touched her where he had not known he wanted to touch her for weeks but now seemed astoundingly clear to him. She sat very straight, her spine rigid, but her eyes were closed and her breaths came quickly, and one hand held a death grip on his shoulder.

"Spread your knees a bit," he said, his voice rockier than he liked.

She did and he dipped deeper. Her back bowed.

"*Oh*." Her fingers dug into his coat.

Oh, indeed. This was what he had intended, and he could bring her release like this; she was taut already, prepared. Yet it wasn't enough for him. He imagined his fingers sliding through her moisture and he ached for it.

"I can do this beneath your skirts if you wish."

"Yes—yes." Her head fell back, her breasts straining at the fabric of her bodice. "Beneath. Yes."

Cam had long been proficient in navigating the labyrinths of feminine skirts. This time it felt like he was uncovering gold—a treasure of inestimable worth—the intimate secrets of a true princess. The fabrics of her garments were thin and fine as he gathered them, revealing slender thighs and the riches at their apex.

"I feel . . ." Her body was rigid. "Exposed."

"You won't feel that in a moment."

"I *am* exposed."

"Only to me, princess. Only ever to me." He drew her mouth beneath his, kissed her softly, and slowly stroked a single fingertip along her aroused flesh.

She moaned, wrapped her hands around his neck, and pressed herself fully into his touch. Here again was the princess he knew, the reserved girl on the outside giving rein to the passionate woman within. She allowed herself the pleasure, thoroughly; indeed she sought it now. He caressed her and with each soft sound of pleasure from her, his control slipped another dangerous notch. He wanted to be inside her. After the endless torture of teasing in her diary, he needed to be inside her. He stroked a circle around her entrance.

"Yes," she panted. "Yes. Please."

He dipped into her. All was hot, wet and soft. So soft. Beautiful. She struggled to take more from him, bearing down on his palm in innocent desperation as though that would suffice. He played with her, giving yet withholding at once, until she was begging with her body. Then he gave her what she wanted, what weeks ago might have been enough for him but now provided him barely an echo of satisfaction, save the satisfaction of knowing he was causing her pleasure. She clutched his shoulders and gave herself fully up to him.

He could have her now, pull her onto his lap and thrust his cock into her and she would accept it. With shoulders thrown back and breasts spilling from her bodice she would ride him like she was riding his fingers, taking him deep and making him forget everything but her. She was passionate, sensual and abandoned.

She came too quickly. He could watch her taking pleasure from him for hours. But her breaths staggered and her muscles convulsed around his fingers and she cried out with a feminine moan of astonishment then pure rapture.

He brought her through it, startling her with the lesson of after-tremors that she had not known to anticipate. Her gasps sounded against his shoulder where she had buried her face, her body shuddering into him as he held her and tried not to feel triumphant or proud or even simply happy. To no avail. He felt it all.

Gradually her breaths slowed and her hands loosened on his coat. She drew away, head bowed, and together they slipped her skirts over her knees once more. With greater discipline than he had ever done anything, he withdrew his arm from around her waist.

Finally she lifted her head, her flushed features set in thoughtful lines.

"That felt even better than I imagined it would." A small smile played about the corner of her rosy lips. If he hadn't been so hard and frustrated and endeavoring with all his might to hide it, Cam might have recognized her words for the greatest compliment a woman had ever given him after sex. The princess's imagination was, after all, extensive.

"It is supposed to feel good, of course." He was astounded at the nonchalance of his voice.

"I am very ..." She glanced aside, the first display of true discomfort she'd shown since he had entered the room. "Damp." She shifted her thighs against each other. Cam swallowed back a groan.

"That is normal. And preferable for actual consumation," he managed to utter, not so nonchalantly now, in fact somewhat strangled. "You may wish to change your chemise."

"I daresay." She looked fully into his eyes. "But first I think you should teach me how to do that to you."

"No!" He jumped up and away from the couch.

"But I need to be able to—"

"This was about you. Not me." *Liar.* Cad. Reprobate.

"But you—"

"I already know what it feels like."

Her lips shut—soft, bruised lips he wanted to kiss again, all day long, and perhaps teach her other activities she might pursue with them. On him. Yes, that was an excellent idea. He would suggest it to her right after he returned from shooting his blackguard self in the heart.

"All right," she said.

All right? He was chagrined to realize that he had hoped she would insist otherwise. But her eyes were remarkably hazy, unconvinced, and that was some consolation at least. "All right."

She stood, shook out her wrinkled skirts, and folded her hands demurely. "Thank you. I feel perfectly prepared now for my . . ." Her cheeks pinkened.

"Wifely duties," he supplied.

Her lips quivered. There was no coquetry about her, and no regret.

"It was . . ." *His pleasure.* More than that. "My pleasure."

"I don't think it was," she said. "But since you will not allow that, I shall have to take your words for the gallantry that they are."

There was nothing gallant about the way he wished to now take her down on that sofa and enact pleasures she had never imagined.

He bowed and tried to grin. "Your highness."

She curtseyed, her smile finally breaking forth. "My lord."

Bemused and still painfully aroused, he left.

When he reached home he went to his study, sat at his desk, and penned seven new stanzas of the poem. Each night the princess escaped her stone tower, feasted with the people of the faery land, sipping of their heady wines, and welcomed the golden prince into her arms and the bed strewn with blossoms while enchanted music wrapped them in a dream of pleasure. When dawn broke, the prince begged her to remain. She could not; the mortal realm pulled her away. As she disappeared into greyness, she glimpsed the sorrow in his eyes, but in her tower she looked from her narrow window into the dull yellow sun of earth and knew that already he had forgotten her.

Cam still had no ending for the poem. But now he knew it would come. Of this, of all in his life, he was certain.

CHAPTER SEVEN

"What are you sewing, Bella?"

Arabella tilted her embroidery frame toward Jacqueline. The pattern was of pirate skulls and crossbones. Jacqueline cracked an inelegant laugh.

"He has a great many cares now as duke," Arabella said. "It is only to make him laugh. He will not wear it."

"I think he will." The duke was besotted with his wife. Indeed, Lord Bedwyr had once assured Jacqueline that his cousin had been besotted from the moment he'd met Arabella. She did not doubt it. Arabella was beautiful, her features perfect, her hair shimmering, and her figure gorgeously proportioned. As unlike Jacqueline as fire and water.

"Perhaps he will wear it in private," Arabella conceded.

Jacqueline now knew that gentlemen did things in private that they would not otherwise admit to.

"Would it be inappropriate for me to give Lord Bedwyr a gift for Christmas?"

Arabella's head snapped up.

"I would like to. Nothing extravagant, of course." Nothing that would match the gift he had given her. That would not be possible and anyway he had already rejected the offer.

They should not have done it. At least she shouldn't have. He, of course, was merely doing what he always did with women. According to all whispered gossip as well as the frank statements of her ladies in waiting, mother, Arabella and the duke, the Earl of Bedwyr was a confirmed rake. Jacqueline had known this since the day they met at the chateau. But also according to reports, he always, without exception, confined his amorous attentions to married women. Several times he had met cuckolded husbands on the dueling field, but he'd never fought a father or brother defending an unwed lady.

Yesterday she had become his single exception.

"We are friends." She willed away the warmth in her cheeks. "Don't friends in your country give each other gifts at Christmastime?"

"Yes." Arabella's brow creased. "But as you are unmarried and he is unmarried—even if he weren't—it would not be proper." She set her embroidery aside. "Jackie, I don't wish to see you hurt."

"I won't be. He has not yet hurt me, though he might have." He might have yesterday. He might have used her thoroughly, as she had secretly wished he would, and then disappeared forever. He had not. Instead, when he encountered her and Reiner riding in the park this morning he'd been the same man she knew well—warm, solicitous, and lightly teasing. After the park he had ridden to the house with them and promised to see her at Lord and Lady Savege's ball tonight. It was as though nothing had happened between them, and perhaps in his estimation nothing had.

"I don't think he will hurt me," she said. "Even if he did, I would not allow it."

"Are you certain? He is, I think, not what you believe him to be. Do you know that he is the man who blinded Luc?"

Jacqueline's heart tripped. "He is?"

"Luc mistakenly accused him of a grievous wrongdoing having to do with his ward, a young girl. Rather than tell his cousin—the closest friend of his life—the truth of it, Cam challenged him to a duel."

A duel?

Arabella nodded. "Neither of them has ever admitted to me whether Cam intended the injury to Luc's eye or whether it was an accident of the moment. But Luc told me he had never seen his cousin so furious."

Jacqueline had never imagined him angry. She didn't know the pleasure-loving nobleman was capable of emotion that strong.

Arabella reached forward and grasped her hand tight. "Dearest friend, take care with him."

Jacqueline nodded. Her throat was tight and words would not come.

After the princess had gone inside the house that morning, Cam had not departed as he fully intended and knew he must. He could not. Seeing her and pretending that all was as it had been was the most difficult challenge he had ever met. But he was happy with the results of his efforts. At first she'd been timid, like the girl he'd first met at the chateau. Shortly, though, she had come out of her shell and fallen back into the easy camaraderie they had lately established.

He should have left when he bid her adieu. Instead he accepted Reiner's invitation to breakfast and, when they were finished—Reiner eating and Cam staring into his coffee—his friend went off to his study to work, and Cam swiftly made his way to the library. What he read there had both astonished him and satisfied his suspicions.

Yesterday and this morning, except for the brief moment of shyness in the park, on the whole she seemed perfectly composed about their encounter—except for the moaning and panting, which was to be expected. She had not, however, seemed generally overcome. To her their intimate commerce had been merely an experiment in confirming the theories she so colorfully depicted in her diary.

To him it had been a revelation.

They were not friends. Now they were lovers and he was glad of it. She, however, had no notion of that or apparently even the desire for it. Her diary entry from the previous day was the tamest, least sensual part of the entire book. It stunned him. She saw him as no other woman ever had—honorable and caring. She believed that in putting her off him that he'd had her best interests in mind and protected her from himself. And perhaps he had. Perhaps in his lust-crazed mind a spark of sanity had urged him to release her before he ruined their friendship. Before he ruined her.

In his chest now swelled an uncomfortably foreign sensation much worse than guilt. She made him want to be the man she imagined. She made him want to be her fantasy—this fantasy—not the godly ravisher but the trusted friend.

Her faith in him humbled him. It also made him angry as hell. How in God's name could she trust him? More importantly, how could she value herself so cheaply that she did not believe she deserved more from him?

They would meet tonight at a ball and he would be obliged to withstand her friendship in the knowledge that friendship was all he would have from her. It was for the best, of course, that they reestablish this footing immediately. Rather, that he did. She apparently already had. The sooner he threw off her fantasies and embraced his reality the better.

When Simms laid out his garments for the evening, Cam studied the black coat and understated waistcoat.

"Simms," he said. "Put these away."

"My lord?"

"Bring me the sapphire velvet, lace cuffs, and diamond buckles." Tonight he would not play the sober landowner responsibly securing his future by wedding a mercenary heiress, but instead the role everyone expected of him: the indolent hedonist without a care in the world. Perhaps if he tried hard enough he would, for a few moments, believe it.

"Tonight?" Jacqueline stood at the side of the crowded ballroom, hands clenched in the fall of her skirts. Until moments ago she had been pleased with those skirts, fashioned from the finest silk and strewn with Mother of Pearl beads and diamond sequins. The gown's delicate bodice and tiny puffed sleeves that miraculously minimized her shoulders, her white satin slippers, the pearls about her throat and the modest tiara nestled in her upswept hair had delighted her too.

Now all her finery felt like a betrayal. Her mother had encouraged the extra time Marguerite had spent at her toilette. The queen had known what Reiner would say to her.

"Maman has grown impatient." He held his voice beneath the music and conversations. "You have had plenty of time to make your decision, Jackie. I must have it by tonight."

"But why this sudden change? You promised I might have until after the holiday."

"It is five days to Christmas. The barons will need time to travel to England for the wedding, as well as the archbishop who wishes to co-officiate."

"Then it seems you have decided for me." She forced her hands to unclench. "It is to be the duke."

"He can do much to aid our country's interests here and abroad. But I won't force you to wed him if you prefer another."

She nodded slowly. "I will marry him, if that is your wish. You have been generous to allow me as much license as you have. Thank you, brother."

He looked as if he wished to say more, then frowned and turned to scan the clusters of guests around them. "Have you seen him?"

She had seen the duke, and as always nothing about him had moved her like even the slightest glance from Lord Bedwyr. "He requested a set."

"Good." Reiner's eyes were troubled. "Perhaps when you dance with him tonight you will show him some of the warmth and animation you reserve for . . . your friends. Ah. There's Liverpool. I've a word to say to him. Do you mind it?"

"Go see the Prime Minister if you must," she said, regretful that as usual her brother felt he must remain at her side. "I will find Arabella."

"You shouldn't wander through this throng alone."

"I can. No one will notice me anyway." She set off through the crowd, slipping between fashionable ladies and gentlemen who as always took no note of her, and came face to face with the Earl of Bedwyr.

"I was looking for you," she said, curtseying.

He bowed elegantly, his dark eyes sparkling. "I could ask for no more melodious greeting."

"Oh, I cannot sing a note."

"I meant the words rather than the intonation."

"I know."

"You can't sing?"

She lifted her brows.

"That bad, hm?" Amusement played at the corner of his mouth that had kissed her with such beauty.

"Like a raven's caw. So, you see, my dreams of singing carols in a red gown must come to naught. Do you sing?"

He looked horrified. "Not if I don't have to."

"When would you have to, I wonder."

"You would be amazed." He was resplendent in a coat of deep blue that shone in the candlelight, a waistcoat embroidered with gold, and a hint of lace stealing from his cuffs. He was the handsomest man in the ballroom and at this moment all his attention was for her. She didn't wonder at the gossip that his former mistresses still held affection for him. He knew precisely how to make a lady feel that she was the only woman in the world.

"Christmas carols, perhaps?" She grinned.

"You jest. But some years back I attended a house party over the holidays at which the guests were required to sing carols every night."

"Every night?"

"After dinner, which was probably a very good thing. By then most of the gentlemen had been drinking for hours. It improved the quality of their song immeasurably."

"I should like a drink right now," she mumbled.

He offered her the most tenderly sympathetic smile that she wanted to reach up and touch his mouth to imprint it upon another of her senses; sight was insufficient.

"Too many people here tonight for my shy princess's tastes?"

Jacqueline's heart did a fluttering skip. *My princess*. Oh, but she understood all those mistresses of his far too well now.

"Actually . . . ." This must be said. "Reiner and my mother have insisted that I choose my husband by the end of the night. I admit to being somewhat apprehensive about it."

Nothing changed in his mien, only the briefest flicker of light in his eyes that might have been the chandelier overhead.

"Ah. I see. Truly cause for imbibing," he said. "And have you?"

"Imbibed? No."

"Chosen."

"Oh. The Duke of Tarleton."

"Tarleton," he said without tone, then as though confounded, "A *duke?*"

She laughed. "It was he or a Prussian general." She shrugged one shoulder lightly and, as once before, his attention seemed to linger there.

"Then you will remain in England after you are wed," he said.

"I will."

He glanced away as though searching for someone, or rather something. Then he looked quite squarely at her before saying, "A drink seems ideal at present."

"There is champagne."

"I said a drink, princess. Not swill. And I suspect you need a stiff brandy as much as I do right about now. Come." He grasped her elbow and led her through the crowded ballroom to a corridor, then through another chamber, charmingly introducing her to other guests as they went, until they reached a closed door. Glancing at the handful of guests nearby, he turned the handle and, with his palm pressing the small of her back, urged her inside.

"How do you know this house so well?" she said when he had turned the key in the lock. The chamber was dark, only moonlight and a low fire in the hearth illuminating his eyes and the dark golden lock that had fallen across his brow.

"Savage and I used to play cards." He moved to a modest sideboard. "What will it be, your highness? Brandy or whiskey? I'm considering having both, so you needn't choose if you don't wish." The heavy *clink* of a carafe sounded against the tabletop, then the softer *clinks* of glasses and the gurgling of liquid.

"I don't think I should have anything." She wandered into the chamber, a music parlor with gilded chairs, a harp, and a pianoforte making dark silhouettes. "Maman will smell it on me."

He came to her and pressed a glass into her palm. "Then you must simply avoid her for the remainder of the night." He tapped his glass to hers. "To you, duchess-to-be." He swallowed the contents in one draught. His broad shoulders seemed to settle and he released a slow breath. He did not move, but looked down at her, his eyes inscrutable. Then he returned to the sideboard and refilled his glass.

Jacqueline sipped her brandy and wondered what her brother would do if he found them in the dark drinking spirits.

"Why did you challenge the Duke of Lycombe to a duel?"

He leaned back against the sideboard. "Did her grace tell you that?" he said over the rim of his glass.

"She did."

He gestured nonchalantly with the glass. "He insulted my fashion sense."

"He did not."

Pushing away from the table, he came toward her. She stepped forward and met him by the pianoforte. Setting down her glass, she opened the keyboard lid and ran her fingertips silently over ivory and ebony.

"You do not sing but you do play," he said and she felt the deep rumble of his voice close to her shoulder in every primed fiber of her body.

She closed the lid. "A princess must learn the musical arts whether she wishes to or not."

"Like she must wed the man her brother and mother choose for her whether she wishes to or not?"

So close, his protective stance was unmistakable. She turned her back to the instrument and placed her palm upon his chest. A thrill of excitement shimmered through her. His heartbeats beneath her hand were quick.

"Your highness." His voice was rough. "I believe I may have made a mistake in encouraging you to drink tonight. I am quite certain it was a mistake for me to have done so."

"I only took one sip."

"One sip is sometimes enough." He did not move away.

She lifted her other hand and ran both of them over his chest and beneath his waistcoat. He allowed it, and she felt every contour of his muscle and strength with her fingertips, as she had dreamed of doing. Heat gathered in her where he had touched her before.

"In the event that I should become betrothed tonight," she said, "and begin the whole bothersome ritual of a formal courtship, I think I need you to give me one more lesson on how to be with a husband."

"Allow me to recall to you the fact that I am not a husband myself." Cam spoke above her brow, the grip he held on his self-control slipping with each pass of her hands across his chest.

Moonlight danced in her eyes. "But you have known plenty of wives."

Who came to him precisely because he did for them what their husbands would not. "Well, I . . ."

"I promise, I only need one more lesson." She pressed onto her toes and kissed his jaw, then his throat, pushing his cravat aside and setting her sweet lips to his skin.

Dragging in deep breaths, he closed his eyes and ran his hands over her back. "Need?"

"Want." Her kisses were soft, fervent and driving him *insane*.

"Princess—"

"Jacqueline."

"Jacqueline, we cannot do this."

"We can."

With a Herculean act of will, he grasped her shoulders and held her off him. "We cannot."

She looked up at him with clear, honest eyes. "Of course we can."

He bent and took her mouth beneath his and kissed her as he had been needing to kiss her since he'd let her out of his arms the day before. Brandy mingled with whiskey and her unique, intoxicating flavor on his tongue as she returned his kisses without a hint of hesitation. She wanted him and he had played into her hands in bringing her here. He'd locked the door, for God's sake, and she hadn't questioned it. That he had wanted this evening to end up this way too only confirmed his depravity twice over.

Her hands upon his chest gave way to her breasts, then the slender length of her body came against him. With their mouths locked, she struggled to get closer, pressing to him, her hands seeking. It wasn't enough for her, and it sure as hell wasn't enough for him. Sliding his hands down her sides, he grasped her hips and lifted her onto the piano top. She wrapped her arms around his neck and welded their mouths together as he pushed up her skirts. Silken stockings became ivory skin and with only her tongue eloquently tangling with his, she invited him to take more of her. He dragged her to him.

She moaned and broke the kiss upon a gasp, but he captured her lips and drank in her astonishment, gripping her hips and rocking her hard against him. Wrapping her legs around his waist, she let him feed his hunger with her sweet body, willingly, wantonly, like the girl in her diary who demanded that he satisfy her.

But this was not satisfaction; it was torture. Too many clothes stood in the way of his hands and mouth. He trailed kisses along her collarbone to the edge of her bodice, and her breasts rose on hard breaths as he drew down the fabric to bare her. *Sweet heaven.* Ivory and rose perfection. Covering one taut peak with his hand, he nipped the other with his teeth.

She gasped, then bit down on her lips to silence herself. Eyes closed, she threaded her fingers through his hair and urged him to her. He licked, tasting the fragrant flavor of her skin, then surrounded the peak with his lips and sucked until she pressed herself hard to his cock. Taking her lips again, with his hands on her hips he ground her against him, seeking satisfaction that could not be had tonight. *Ever.*

"My God," he whispered. "What I could demand of you now . . . What I could ask you to do to me, and you would allow it."

"I would. I would do whatever you wished." Her mouth traveled along his jaw. "But you will not ask me."

He pulled her off him. Her eyes were half-lidded yet glimmering with awareness.

"How do you know I won't?" he demanded.

"You are the only one who understands me. You are the only one who does not judge me for what I am not, or ask of me what I am not willing to give."

"A man with a black heart cannot very well judge a girl with a diamond soul."

"Diamonds are cold and hard. And you are not black-hearted. You are gold." She ran her fingers through his hair. "You are sun."

Her diary. His poem. He didn't know which was which now, where they ended and reality began. "Don't confuse what you see with what lies beneath, princess."

"You cannot lie to me, my lord." Her fingertips slipped over his lips, caressing so gently, so softly. "I know you."

His heart beat irregularly fast. "Then you know that I am a magnificent dancer."

Her brow wrinkled. "Dancer?"

He forced himself to draw away from her, to rearrange her skirts about her knees. "I am particularly fond of the waltz. Of course." He offered her a wicked grin and stroked the silk into place over her hips, not allowing himself to linger.

"Are you?" She sounded bewildered.

He lifted her off the piano and released her. But he remained close, knowing it must end, forever this time, but unable to end it quite yet. "I am. And I should like to waltz with you now."

"Oh."

"Don't sound so disappointed. Ladies vie for the opportunity to waltz with me. Now, I beg you, precede me from this chamber and I will meet you shortly without."

"But why—"

"I require a moment to compose myself."

She glanced down at his evident discomposure and a

tremulous smile caught at the corner of her mouth. She went to the door and turned the key. Then she paused and looked over her shoulder, a thoughtful frown tugging at her brow. "There will be no more lessons, then, I am to understand?"

He knew what he should say.

"If you require further instruction, princess, I am at your disposal." He could never deny her. He bowed.

When the door shut with a click he groaned and wished for a cold bath and a pistol to aim at his heart.

Lord Bedwyr returned to the ballroom as Duke Tarleton was approaching her to claim his waltz. Jacqueline dragged her attention away from the earl and gave it to the man who would soon be her husband.

The duke bowed stiffly. "Your highness, you look well this evening."

She *felt* well. The whole world must be able to see how well.

"Shall we?" He gestured to couples taking their places to dance and offered his arm.

"Go away, Tarleton." Lord Bedwyr's deep voice came at her shoulder. "You'll have your chance soon enough." He did not take her hand but swept her into his arms and danced her away.

She craned her neck. The duke stared after them grimly.

"Why did you do that?" She struggled not to smile from all the pleasure tangled inside her. "He reserved this set with me."

"I cannot abide dukes," he said easily. "Especially the

stiff-necked, serious variety. Far too confident of themselves. Couldn't you have chosen the Prussian instead?"

"The general is stiff-necked and serious too. And for you to chastise another man for over-confidence seems outrageously disingenuous, my lord."

"Didn't Reiner come up with any other foreign candidates? A Russian count? Or perhaps a Turkish vizier?"

"I thought you liked it that I will remain in England after I wed."

His hand tightened upon her waist. "I'm thinking that might not be entirely a good thing after all."

The heat of something that was not pleasure—shame, or perhaps despondency—crawled into her cheeks.

"Lady Amelia Whitley is very lovely," she made herself say.

The light in his eyes sharpened. "I'm enjoying these non sequiturs, less than usual this evening, I must admit."

But this must be said. "I cannot imagine that you would worry you could be unfaithful to her."

"I have no concern on that issue," he said firmly.

"I did not mean to insult you. It is only that everybody says—"

"I have never been with more than one woman at a time."

"Each affair lasting a day."

Abruptly, he laughed. "You are far too cynical for one so young."

"I am a realist. And I am observant."

He glanced at the guests on the peripheries of the dance floor. "Observing from a distance can lead to inaccurate conclusions." His gaze returned to hers and she could not read what she saw in it.

"I needn't observe from a distance. Two nights ago at the Thornes' party, Lady Patterson was weeping in the ladies' retiring room over her husband's infidelity with yet another mistress."

His eyes widened. "She said this to you?"

"To Mrs. Phelps."

"In your presence?"

"They did not notice I was there. Ladies rarely do. Or they imagine that because they have never heard me speak I am unable to understand English. The consequence is that I hear quite a lot more than they know. It was much the same when I went about with Reiner in Paris. So you see, I am privy to the realities of gentlemen of high society. They are often disloyal to their wives, and sometimes vice versa."

He remained silent a moment, his strength and grace carrying her through the dance as though it was his sole desire to give her joy in this moment.

"I would be faithful to my wife," he said.

She tried to laugh. But he was not laughing, nor even smiling. Instead his hand tightened about hers and his fingers upon her back spread.

He was not speaking of her. He could not be speaking of her, of course. But Jacqueline allowed herself for a moment to pretend that he was. He drew her closer and she tried not to smile in pure happiness but everyone in the place must see it shining through her. It burst from her fingertips and tumbled out her eyes and she could not stanch it.

When the dance ended, he led her to the duke.

"Take care of her, Tarleton," he said. "She deserves a

prince." He took her hand and kissed it, and then with a smile he strolled away.

Jacqueline danced and made pleasantries with the duke. He was inclined to talk and as she was inclined to the opposite she thought that they would get along very well. But she did not want to simply get along. She wanted to *live*. When the set ended, she claimed to have seen her good friend the Duchess of Lycombe going off into another chamber, and she slipped away from him.

She found a potted plant in the corner to hide behind and looked for the earl in the crowd. He stood with a cluster of ladies and gentlemen.

He glowed.

She knew that his blond beauty did not actually glow. But as he laughed with others and enjoyed himself, he shone like gold and she felt it inside her. For all his gorgeous popularity, she had a part of him. She was not fool enough to believe he did not share kisses and caresses with other women. But she had his friendship, and dancing in his arms, for the first time in her life she'd felt like a fairytale princess.

"Silly foreign girl. Did you see the way she was staring at him? Positively besotted." A giggle followed this comment confided on the other side of the potted plant.

"Perhaps she hasn't any notion of his reputation," another feminine voice whispered.

"He is an incorrigible flirt," the first one said.

"He cannot even resist flirting with a girl like *her*."

"She is a princess, Marissa. She must be worth a fortune, and everybody knows Bedwyr is nearly broke."

"Of course, Delilah. But can you imagine Cam Westfall

caring about a lady's fortune if it isn't attached to a pretty face and *ample* other attractions?"

"Ample! Oh, Marissa, you are a wit."

"Truly, he should not tease her. A girl like that is bound to misconstrue his attentions. She will get horridly hurt."

"Wounded."

"Damaged."

"Devastated."

"Demolished."

It sounded like they relished her inevitable heartbreak. Jacqueline considered finding the library and bringing them a dictionary in case they ran out of words to describe it.

Stepping out from behind the plant she gave the pair a regal nod and with her shoulders back glided away from them. When she found her mother, the queen's eyes were glittering with displeasure.

"Stroll with me, daughter."

Jacqueline fell into step beside her. She suspected what was to come, but where before she always dreaded conversations like this, now she did not. She could not apologize for her happiness.

"Now that you will be betrothed to the duke, you must avoid Lord Bedwyr."

"What? No preamble, Maman?" she asked lightly. "Am I not to have a lecture on proper comportment in public before you deliver your principal chastisement?"

Her mother's eyes snapped. "You demean yourself by encouraging his flirtations."

"I demean myself by enjoying the friendship of a handsome, popular lord? Good gracious, society here has high standards."

"Beside him your lack of beauty is pronounced."

Jacqueline felt the words in her belly. "Then in the future I must make certain to become friends with only plain gentlemen."

Her mother came to a halt. "Have you given your consent to Reiner to wed Tarleton?"

Her nerves raced. "Maman, I do not wish to wed Duke Tarleton. Or General Von Franck or Prince Sebastiao. I do not wish to wed anyone and I don't see why I must. Reiner helped negotiate the Treaty of Paris not two years ago with enormous success. Sensaire will not suffer for lack of allies if I do not marry. Our barons don't like the idea of a foreign lord with influence in our kingdom anyway."

"What do you know of the needs of our kingdom?"

"Everything. Every day Reiner tells me of his concerns and troubles. I am his closest companion, his best friend, and I cannot believe that he would be forcing me into marriage unless you were pressuring him to do so. But you are not the ruler of our kingdom. You cannot dictate my brother's decisions." She was trembling, but the words tasted wonderful.

The queen's eyes narrowed. "Unfortunately, your brother's impatience to see you wed has more to do with his friend's marked interest in you than with the needs of our kingdom."

Jacqueline's breath shot out of her. "What?"

"Reiner knows the earl will not offer for you. Lord Bedwyr is using you."

She shook her head. "For what?"

"For your naïveté."

"If so, he is welcome to it. For I don't want it any longer."

"He will hurt you, Jacqueline."

They were Arabella's words, and Jacqueline swallowed back her fear. "I am finished speaking with you about this, Maman." She turned away and sought out her brother in the crowd.

CHAPTER EIGHT

Cam left the ball the moment after he gave the princess into
Tarleton's hands, and found Tony at his club. There he got
drunk—as drunk as he had once considered getting when
he'd first read a lady's diary and imagined it to be the only way
to deflect her infatuation. He did not, however, do anything
particularly embarrassing. Instead, when they'd emptied too
many bottles to count he dismissed his carriage, walked home
in a black cloud, and as the dawn crept through the draperies
he fell onto his bed fully clothed.

He awoke to his valet hovering above him.

"My lord, her ladyship awaits you in the parlor."

Cam scrubbed his hands over his face. Cracking his
eyes open, he surveyed his crushed coat and single shoe *sans*
diamond buckle. But he had no further use for such finery
anyway. He was about to become a respectably struggling
farmer in Devonshire. Those sorts of fellows didn't wear
velvet and diamonds. At least he didn't think so.

He would soon find out.

"Tell her ladyship to go to the devil," he grumbled.

"She refuses to leave until she has spoken with you." Simms offered him a damp linen cloth from which lemony steam arose.

Cam grimaced. "What in the devil is this?"

"Step one of your recovery, my lord."

He submitted to his valet's ministrations and within too short a time was dressed and stumbling down the stairs. His head ached and he was still three quarters foxed, but this interview must be gotten over with.

Lady Rowdon stood in the center of the parlor.

"My lady." A deep bow nearly toppled him over.

"This delay is unacceptable, Bedwyr. You will call upon my goddaughter and offer for her today or I will cut you from my last testament."

"I am devastated to be obliged to inform you, Great-auntie, that your program does not suit me after all. I find I cannot wed where I am not inclined." He couldn't wed where he was inclined either. But bachelorhood was a state he knew well, and cousin Herbert or Fitzherbert or whoever it was would be thrilled to inherit the earldom.

The black feather atop Lady Rowdon's bonnet quivered with the suppressed outrage in her tiny frame. "You will not have Aylesley."

"Then I will not have it." He shrugged a shoulder and wished he had Jacqueline's knack for making the gesture seem at once innocent and wise. "Easy come, easy go." His gut and head ached so hard he thought that if he didn't sit down soon he might indeed fall over. How on earth had he lost his head for liquor?

A month spent in the company of a maidenly princess.

It had been worth it.

"Don't think you will purchase Aylesley from me." Spots of color had risen in his great-aunt's ashen cheeks. She was in a rare pelter.

"You have already made it clear that option was not on the table."

"If it were, you would never be able to raise the funds. You would attempt it at the tables and fail just as your father always did, the profligate wastrel."

Cam had heard it all before. "Your point, madam?"

"My niece was ruined the day she wed him. Yet you—her only joy and hope—have made yourself his heir in every way," she spat, but moisture stained her eyes.

All at once Cam felt preternaturally alert and as though time had ceased marching forward. *She wanted him to have Aylesley.*

"If I could raise the money without gambling, and without depleting Crofton," he said slowly, "would you sell Aylesley to me?"

"You cannot. You will not."

From the old termagant this was tantamount to assent. Cam's head spun.

"If you will excuse me, madam," he said with another bow that nearly toppled him over. "I must take my leave of you now. My butler will see you out. Good day."

He wasted no time having his solicitor summoned, but stopped in his study to gather a leather satchel, then rode to Smythe's office.

"My lord!" The solicitor leaped to his feet.

"What, Smythe?" Cam drawled because it was somewhat easier than enunciating syllables. How many bottles of brandy had Tony plied him with, for God's sake? "Didn't my father ever visit you here? For an emergency loan off the estate, perhaps?"

Smythe cleared his throat uncomfortably. "Perhaps three or four times, my lord."

"Rest easy. I haven't come for that." He sat in the chair across the desk and folded his hands. "But I do need funds. How much in liquid assets can I have now without causing Crofton to suffer in any manner?"

"In any manner, my lord?"

"Down to the smallest lamb and most ramshackle wheelbarrow."

Smythe opened a leger, scribbled numbers in it, and named a sum. It wasn't quite enough.

Cam stood. "Make the funds available in my bank. But not a penny more, do you understand?"

"Yes, my lord."

His next destination was mere blocks away. Snatching the satchel from his saddle, he entered the modest offices of Brittle & Sons, Printers, and produced his card. The clerk at the desk fell over himself offering tea and a comfortable chair. In desperate need of both after riding across half of London, with his head splitting, Cam asked to immediately meet with one of the Mr. Brittles, preferably the elder.

The elder Mr. Brittle was a watery-eyed fellow with a substantial belly, a thick gold watch chain, and a signet ring the size of the Tower of London on his middle finger. Clearly he was well heeled. Cam produced the contents of the satchel and made his offer.

Brittle did not go so far as to lick his lips, but he did rub his hands together. Cam was satisfied with the price offered, sufficient in addition to the funds from Crofton to make Lady Rowdon a respectable offer on Aylesley.

By the time the documents were signed and all settled, he needed a place to lie down more than even a house in Kent. Doing his best to appear threatening and probably making a half-drunken hash of it, he said, "It requires minor edits before the final printing, and of course it lacks an ending as yet. When I've finished it, I will send it via courier."

"The day after tomorrow, my lord?"

"Fine." He'd nothing better to do—except sleep—and the sooner the money came into his hands the sooner he would have Aylesley. The changes to the poem would be slight, in any case. He would make the faery prince a dark fellow, black hair, pale skin and eyes like a silver brook or some such thing. Perfectly reasonable for a faery prince. The human princess would become an insipid blonde. Nothing would remain in the final version that would cause his real princess to suspect the poem had anything to do with her, not even his name upon it.

The author would be "A Gentleman of Quality." Brittle already published leaflets penned by an anonymous lady rabble-rouser who went by the name Lady Justice, and he made guineas hand over fist from her. His society readers would go mad trying to discover the identity of the anonymous author of *The Stone Princess*. But by the time the poem was published, Cam would already be in Paris collecting Claire and preparing for her move to Aylesley. He would settle her there first, then he would retire to Crofton and drink a carafe of brandy daily so as not to ever have to suffer this weak head again.

He shook Brittle's outstretched hand, mounted his horse, and headed for his great-aunt's house.

Cam slept hard and awoke shortly after dawn. Before knowing the Princess of Sensaire, sleeping through the day had been his usual habit. Anything to avoid restless idleness. Those days were over now, the last distracting debauchery out of his blood. He had two estates and a twelve-year-old girl to care for; plenty of distraction to fill his hours.

Clearing his head with coffee, he settled at his desk to make the necessary changes to the poem. The footman entered with breakfast and the post, and before setting to his task Cam filed through the correspondence, discarding invitations to Christmas parties. Lingering in London would be foolish and accomplish nothing. He would set off for Paris at once.

A light feminine hand had scrolled his name familiarly across a note written on scented paper. Lady Flint had been fond of sending him notes via her page boy, but she hadn't done so in years. He leaned back in his chair and snapped the wax seal on the letter.

Darling, if you were looking for company you might have come see me.

He could almost hear her lush chuckle he'd once found so entrancing.

But I jest. Lord Abernathy tells me the wager in the betting book at his club is already eight-to-one that she is the

*author, not you, despite the attribution. Poor little foreign
mouse. I have always said that you are as bittersweet an
affliction to a lady as opium.*

*Do pay me a call if you should wish for more experienced
mortal companionship.*

—M

Enclosed in the missive was a cheaply produced printed
sheet about half the size of a regular broadsheet. But it
did not contain the usual scandalous gossip and crimes
found on such publications. Instead, the first two-dozen
stanzas of *The Stone Princess* stared back at Cam. Unedited.
Unaltered.

Heart pounding, immobile, he stared at the paper. Then,
stuffing it into his pocket, he bolted from his chair.

The princess would not see him. Cam stood upon the door-
step of Reiner's house and resisted pleading with the butler.

Instead he went to Brittle & Sons. Early afternoon sun
cast crisp winter shadows over the east side of town where
commerce and traffic bustled. But the door to the printer's
shop was locked fast. A sign nailed to it read: *Barraged by demands for Part II of The Stone Princess, Brittle & Sons is closed
to the public in order to set the next chapters.*

Closed to the Earl of Bedwyr, more likely.

He would murder Brittle. Why the blackguard had pre-
maturely published the thing, Cam couldn't fathom, unless
he supposed that after the holiday fewer members of society
would be in town to purchase it.

He returned home to find his receiving table littered with calling cards and notes, including a message from Reiner. The note said he hadn't sufficient evidence to conclude that Cam was the author of the poem, and Jacqueline would not speak of it. He could not believe Cam would do such a thing, but he was angry nonetheless for the embarrassment Cam had exposed her to by paying her so much attention. That scandalmongers and gossips were seizing upon the likeness of the stone princess and faery prince to his sister and friend because of Cam's marked attention to her over the past several weeks was his and Cam's fault alone, yet she was the one suffering from it. Reiner closed with the request that he not call at the house until this had all blown over.

Cam swallowed hard against his rising panic. That society had in a single day made this its favored scandal did not trouble him. He had often before been the center of such attention. But that Jacqueline would not speak of it to her brother made his blood cold. The woman he knew, the clever, passionate woman who had given herself shamelessly to him would not shrink from being mistaken for a character in a work of fiction. She would face it with dignity and grace, and she would laugh with him about it. That she refused to speak with Reiner could have only one explanation.

She knew.

He uncrumpled the broadsheet and reread the stanzas. And there, in black ink, were her diary entries. He had embellished, translated them into verse, invented another world into which the princess went each night. But at heart it was her story—a story of loneliness and awakening.

How could he have been such a fool?

He pulled out a sheet of stationery and wrote to her. If she would not see him, she must read his apology. He sent a footman with it to her house.

The note came back to him unopened.

He could not remain still. He ordered Saladin saddled then left the horse in the stable and set out on foot. Standing before his club he wanted with every fiber to walk inside and get rip roaring foxed. But he'd been foxed when he had foolishly left the poem with Brittle the day before. Not only foxed, he understood now. Devastated. Aylesley was to be his but she was not. She was to be a duchess, and he was to retreat to the country where he would never be obliged to encounter her and have it borne in upon him what a blind fool he was.

He walked aimlessly until dark, and when the lamplighters went about illuminating the streets, he continued walking. He did not stop walking until daylight broke. Returning home, he slept fitfully for an hour. By nine o'clock found himself on the threshold of his cousin's house. Luc met him in the parlor.

"You look like hell," Luc said, scanning him. "You've read the poem, I assume?"

"I've read it."

"You wrote it."

"I did."

"God damn it, Cam. Of all the women you might have—"

"I never intended this. Of course I didn't."

Luc studied him. "What do you want from me?"

"I don't want anything from you. I came here to speak with your wife."

"I don't know that she will see you. She spent last evening with Jacqueline."

Cam's gut was hollow. "Is Arabella awake?"

"Cam." Luc's brow was tight. "Reiner and Tarleton signed the marriage contract yesterday. Jacqueline is betrothed."

There it was. If he were lucky, he could hope for no more than forgiveness, someday, and even then from a distance.

Now, however, at least he could stop more of the poem from being distributed. Leaving his cousin's house, he went to Brittle & Sons. The door was still bolted. The sign now read: *Part II of* The Stone Princess *AVAILABLE TOMORROW!*

Returning home he penned a letter of threat and sent his footman with it to the publisher. The polite reply he received indicated that if he did not provide a suitable ending to the poem before the following day, the contract would be null and void and all proceeds from the sale of Parts I and II of *The Stone Princess* would revert to Brittle & Sons, Printers. With an economy of words, Cam replied that it would be a chilly day in hell. Then he saddled Saladin himself and rode to her house.

The royal family was out, the butler informed him, adding that he had been instructed to deny Lord Bedwyr entrance on all occasions.

As martial pastimes went, Cam had always preferred elegant swordplay. At this moment, however, he came to understand that uniquely masculine urge to hit something very hard with his fists. He went to the boxing club but there he swiftly discovered that society did indeed believe the princess had written the poem. He was able to endure the suggestive ribbing of his opponent at her expense for all of one minute.

Then he swung with such force that the man's nose broke. Cam left the ring, a chorus of epithets in his wake that he barely heard.

The following morning he received a call from the one person he did not mind admitting to his house. Tony Masinter settled into a chair across the dining table and informed him that town was abuzz with news of a remarkable poem. Brittle & Sons had allowed the information to "leak" that the gentleman author of *The Stone Princess* was refusing to complete his masterpiece and subsequently would not be paid.

"Princess, hm?" the naval captain said, twirling a long black moustache.

Cam lifted a brow.

Tony chuckled. "I'm not such a noddycock, Charles, that I haven't noticed your absence this past month. No cards. No tables of any sort. No Madam Patrice. No fun. And now the poem. Ergo, princess."

"You are not as foolish as you look, Anthony."

"Don't see why you're not crowing over your success. That poem is all anybody can talk about."

Cam sank his head into his hands.

"I'm guessing she don't like the thing," Tony said.

"You're guessing right."

A lengthy silence ensued. Tony snapped his fingers. "I know what. Why don't you write the ending you think she'd like best?"

Cam's head jerked up. "I could kiss you, Anthony."

"Don't," the captain replied with a jaunty grin. "Just oiled the moustaches, don't you know. Wouldn't want to muss them up."

After two days, the icy-hot devastation Jacqueline suffered the moment she understood what he'd done had become an aching sorrow, and anger at her own foolishness. Unlike everybody else, she had no doubt as to the poem's authorship. No one knew how closely the story followed her diary entries. No one but him, apparently.

As she had used him to fuel her fantasies, he had also used her. Whether he had found her diary recently or long ago, she did not wish to know. Both possibilities left her heart battered. That he needed the money he would earn from the poem to maintain his mode of living had become clear to her. Arabella said that he worked diligently to restore the estate his father had depleted, but that did not suffice. His marriage to Lady Amelia Whitley would bring him sufficient funds to repair Crofton and continue to live in style in town, and it would endear him to his wealthy great-aunt.

But no betrothal announcement between the Earl of Bedwyr and the daughter of the Earl of Maythorpe came. Gossip from Marguerite, carried through servants' channels, had it that the match had come to nothing. Only Jacqueline knew why. While society believed her to be filling her purse with guineas earned from the overnight popularity of *The Stone Princess*, she knew who was benefiting from it.

Now, however, the publisher had announced that the author refused to produce the final stanzas and would not be paid for any of it. No one had more reason than her to wish that an ending would never be printed. She ought to despise him. She ought to wish him to the devil. But she was discovering that love did not diminish simply because a person wished it. That he had used her abominably did not make her heart any less raw. And she was at fault too; she never should have written that diary. The secrets in it had unbound her confidence, but falsely. She had pretended friendship with him when she had dreamed so ardently of more.

Now, one final piece of fiction must bring to a close the fantasy. It would be the only response she would give to him for what he had done, and it suited her.

Sitting down to her writing table, she drew from the drawer the first two parts of his poem, her diary, and a fresh leaf of paper. She was no poet, but the couplets came fluidly. Reality was even easier to write than fantasy, it seemed. Finally, she wiped the tears from her cheeks, folded the pages, and called for a carriage.

Brittle & Sons was little more than a shop front quivering with the rattle of a press in a nearby room. The clerk peered out the window at her carriage and promptly escorted her to his employer.

She gave Mr. Brittle the pages. He scanned them at first desultorily, then eagerly. He glanced up at her then flipped the page. His head bobbed. "The cruel old king finally orders his daughter to marry a mortal knight," he said.

"She is resigned to her mortal life and agrees."

"Yes, yes." His eyes were bright. "She says nothing so that in the faery world the sun prince can wed the faery heiress—" His gaze flicked up to her for an instant. "That is to say, the faery princess meant for him."

"He forgets about the mortal princess entirely. For in the land of faery, time is nothing and beauty and joy are all." Heat was gathering again at the back of her eyes. "Will you accept these as the completion of *The Stone Princess*, Mr. Brittle?"

He pursed his lips and his gaze flicked between her and the pages in his hands. "You want nothing for these?"

"Only a promise that you will pay the original author the promised price for the entire poem."

A moment passed, then another.

"I will do it." This time his nod was a bow. "Your highness."

She swallowed her surprise. What had she suspected? Everyone knew the partial truth already. Now this man knew her truth.

Ducking her head, she went out of the shop. Mr. Brittle had what he wanted: an ending to the poem. The earl had what he wanted: funds to enable him not to wed. And she had what she did not want but what she needed: an end to fantasy. An end to dreams. Reality once more. This time forever.

CHAPTER NINE

Cam dragged himself from sleep and surveyed the destruction around him. His desk was strewn with crumpled paper, an inkbottle overturned, and at least six pens lay broken over the walnut surface. But the poem was finished.

Gathering the pages, he tucked them into his pocket, ran a hand through his hair to untangle it, and buttoned his coat.

Riding beneath the darkening sky, snow flurries settling upon his shoulders, he was at the printer's shop within thirty minutes. Mr. Brittle greeted him with a curious brow.

"Here is the ending." Cam thrust the pages at him. "Now print it and be done with it."

"But, my lord—"

"I don't care about the money. In fact, damn you and your greedy soul, Brittle. I don't want a penny of it. But if you do not print this tomorrow, I will have your head on a post on my gate, mark my words."

"But, my lord, Part III of *The Stone Princess* is already in production."

"It can't be. I've only just finished it."

"Yet it is." Brittle's head bobbed like a wooden duck's. "It was delivered this afternoon. I instructed the pressmen to set it immediately. So, you see, I won't need this." He extended the pages to Cam.

Blurry-eyed, Cam stared. "It is the work of an imposter."

"If so, it's a very good imposter, my lord. You won't be disappointed."

"*No*," Cam ground out and pushed his pages back at him. "Print this, Brittle, or so help me . . ."

The man held his palms up. "I beg your pardon, my lord. Time is money in the printing business, and I haven't the time to reset this. Tomorrow is Christmas Eve. Everybody will be clamoring to have Part III before they head off to their parties. By nightfall three-quarters of London will be reading the enthralling final act of *The Stone Princess*. You cannot ask me to disappoint your adoring readers, can you?"

"If you print the imposter's version, they won't be my adoring readers, but *his*," he growled.

Brittle shook his head ruefully.

Cam damned him, twice, aloud, left the pages on the table, and stalked out of the shop. But he blamed himself. An eleventh-hour solution was no solution at all. He had hurt her and he must simply bear the consequences of it. For a lifetime.

Josiah Brittle, printer and sometimes publisher, had never considered himself a particularly sentimental sort. He was a working man, and he hadn't been born with a silver spoon in his mouth. He had earned every shilling through sweat and labor. Occasionally he'd had to make unsavory decisions in order to turn a profit.

But as he scanned the Earl of Bedwyr's scrawled verses, something stirred in his old heart, something that recalled years past when he'd first met the girl who had stolen that heart. Even though she'd been nothing more than a seamstress in a dress shop, he had fallen on his rear when she spoke to him. Starved with calf-love, he'd been willing to do anything to have that girl.

He saw that in the pages in his hands.

He also saw guineas. Sacks of guineas. All of London would be talking about this by Christmas morning. With the money it brought in, he would be able to buy that girl from years ago, now Mrs. Brittle, that brooch she'd been wanting.

Also—and not to be discounted to a man who valued quality—his lordship's poetry was considerably better than her highness's.

He strode into the pressroom and handed the pages to the pressmen. They scurried to obey. Josiah Brittle nodded in satisfaction. This would be a happy Christmas indeed.

The room was festive, draped with evergreen boughs and glittering with candles and elegant people, the aromas of cinnamon, cloves and mulled wine wafting all about. Jacqueline folded her hands in her lap, closed her eyes, and allowed the holiday cheer to ebb around her. That the musicians seemed to be fixed on playing carols, which put her in mind of the single person she did not wish to think about, must be endured.

She had come to this grand Christmas Eve party in the full awareness that she would be stared at, whispered about, and pitied. Her expectations were met. Part III of the poem had appeared on street corners in the early afternoon. Everybody at the party had already read it. Their burning curiosity to know whether she had also read it was palpable.

But she had taken measures against this. Beneath her fingers the stiff red satin of her gown crackled. Her shoulders were cold—a consequence of baring them entirely—but she held them straight and confident. The Earl of Bedwyr's betrayal had one positive effect: she needn't hide any longer. For even when she hid she was exposed. So, exposed she would be again, but now by her own choice, and she would revel in it even if her insides were quaking.

Arabella slipped into the chair beside her. "Jackie—"

"Look at those women over there, Bella. They haven't ceased staring at me all night. One would think they'd never seen a fictional character come to life before."

"They and everybody else," Arabella said impatiently. "But not for— Jackie, are you listening to me?"

"And that Baron whatever-his-name-is has winked at me six times. Six! Can you imagine? It is positively diverting."

"Jackie, look at me." Arabella held a cheaply printed broadsheet. "Have you read this? Part III?"

"I have. It is a very satisfying finale."

"*Satisfying?*"

"Everybody ends up just as they should," she forced herself to say.

Arabella squeezed her hand. "This is not like you, darling.

He hurt you terribly, and I understand that this ending satisfies that hurt. But you cannot like the stone princess's fate. Do not tell me you have resigned yourself to it."

"I haven't, of course. She goes willingly, while I—"

"Willingly?" Arabella peered at her. "You haven't read it, have you?" She pressed the page into her palm.

Jacqueline cared nothing that at least a dozen pairs of eyes were on her as she uncreased the paper and yet again forced her misery behind the blockade of pride and confidence she had erected. If they must all see her read it to be satisfied she knew the ending—the ending she had written an hour after telling Duke Tarleton that she could not marry him or any other man—then so be it.

But as her eyes scanned the words, she did not recognize them. This was not her writing.

> *The king he swore in fury's rage*
> *His daughter would be wed*
> *To warlike man through violent force,*
> *And chained to mortal bed.*

> *The princess wed; her husband learned*
> *The secret of the portal.*
> *With axe and club he broke it down,*
> *Entrapping her as mortal.*

> *The Sun Prince knew not this tragic fate;*
> *He waited at the feast.*
> *'Midst song and dance he watched for her,*
> *Yet found in them no peace.*

Kisses, She Wrote 151

In silv'ry light he stood upon
The brook's clear bank where once
With hands entwined they'd spoke of joy,
Yet now came still silence.

Days passed to weeks, weeks into months.
The princess did not come.
He called his heartbreak to the stars,
Beneath which they had loved.

The trees whispered his sorrow's grief,
The Moon in solace shone,
But the prince no comfort would he take
Now his mortal maid was gone.

His beauty waned; the prince grew weak.
His golden luster faded.
For it was she who'd brought him life;
From her his beauty came.

O'er song and feast the dark night crept
Upon the desolate shore.
Then sending forth his final breath,
The Sun Prince was no more.

Jacqueline blinked, shedding a tear and marring the freshly printed ink. She swiped a finger beneath her lashes. Before her appeared a linen kerchief. The hand that held it was masculine, strong and familiar. She lifted her head.

The Earl of Bedwyr knelt before her upon one knee. His

hair was tousled, his coat wrinkled, his cravat hastily tied, and his hand extending the linen was unsteady. His dark eyes spoke something she could not readily believe: hope.

"Princess." His voice was rough. "Don't let me die."

There was nothing to be said, only the happiness she had dreamed now to be seized. But the hurt was too fresh. She brandished the broadsheet. "I admit, my lord, that your theory about Christmas gifts chosen to suit the recipient for greatest effect has merit."

"Only if the effect is to inspire mercy," he replied quietly.

She could not bear the confusion. She dipped her gaze. "When?" she whispered.

"At the chateau."

Her eyes came up. "At first?"

"I was intrigued. I had never known a woman like you." His throat moved awkwardly. "I came to understand that there are no others."

The page crinkled between her fingers. "Why did you do it?"

"Because I wanted you, and I think I didn't know how to have you otherwise. Jacqueline, I have been a great fool, but I never wished to hurt you. I beg of you, if you can someday forgive m—"

Her palm upon his chest stayed his words. Then she leaned forward, released a shaking breath, and buried her face in his shoulder. He wrapped his arms about her and held her tight.

"I assume from this response that you will not, after all, be marrying Tarleton?" he said into her hair.

"I will not. I could not." Tears of joy arose in her eyes and soaked his shoulder.

He stroked her hair. "Then perhaps you might consider marrying me instead? If you don't, you know, you will never live this down, embracing a man with a hundred people looking on."

"*Are* they looking?"

"Yes. I think they're all eager to hear you sing 'God Rest Ye, Merry Gentlemen.' I know I am."

"Is there perhaps a black veil lying anywhere about?"

"No, but I could remove my coat and you could throw that over your head. No one would recognize you, I'm certain."

She laughed and he held her tighter yet.

"My darling," he whispered close. "My love."

Finally she lifted her head and looked into his eyes, and her heart danced.

His gaze slipped downward. "Nice gown. Red, hm?"

"You ruined me."

He lifted a brow. "Not quite as thoroughly as I would have liked to, in truth. But—"

"Red seemed the only alternative to shutting myself up in a stone tower for the remainder of my life, and so much more fun anyway." She tucked her hand into his. "But this is even more fun. Considerably more, really."

His smile was like the sun. He kissed her there, a kiss of promise and passion and tender delight. And because she had not answered him the first time, he asked again for her hand. She gave it. Then in a whisper only he could hear, she offered him the rest of herself as well. As a Christmas gift.

EPILOGUE

Jacqueline sank back into the mattress, struggling for breath.

Cam lifted his head. "Good lord," he uttered, his chest moving hard. "We should have done that weeks ago."

She ran her hands along his arms that were hard with muscle and damp from his exertion. "Weeks ago I was a wallflower and you were a libertine."

"Weeks ago I was a frustrated celibate made mad by the writings of a lusty innocent."

She threaded her fingers into his hair and pulled him down to kiss her.

"But no more," he murmured against her lips. "In fact . . ." He drew away, laying kisses upon her throat, her breast and belly as he went. He shrugged a dressing gown over his shoulders and Jacqueline reveled at the sight. Always she reveled these days. There seemed no end to it.

Opening a drawer, he drew forth her diary. As he flipped through the pages she curled into the soft bed linens and watched him.

"Aha." Finger upon a page, he looked over to her. "This."

"This?" she said languorously. It wasn't three o'clock in the afternoon and yet here they were again. If their servants told anyone how often Lord and Lady Bedwyr retired to the master's bedchamber during the daylight hours they would have yet more gossip on their hands—gossip Jacqueline would bear with pride.

Her husband stretched himself out beside her. "This," he repeated, positioning the page so she could read it. She scanned her own prose, too replete and happy to blush.

"Oh, that," she said, smiling.

"How on earth did you know anything about *that?*" he said, pinning her with warm interest.

She trailed a fingertip down his chest. "My imagination is remarkably creative when suitably inspired."

He set the book aside and slipped his hand along her thigh. "Shall we reward your imagination for its superb creativity?"

She ran her palms over his shoulders, dislodging the dressing gown. "Do you want to do *that,* my lord?"

"I intend to do that, your highness." His voice came huskily in her ear, his hand upon her making her sigh.

"I suppose I am your Muse, after all."

"You are my Muse," he concurred, "and must be obeyed."

She wrapped her arms around his neck and arched to him. "Let the fantasy begin."

Author's Note

Inspiration for Cam's poetry came to me via Byron, Shelley, Wordsworth and Coleridge — the titans of Romantic-era poetry. While I cannot claim to be a poet (and I beg forgiveness of my readers with discerning tastes in verse), I'll admit that I had a whole lot of fun writing the brief sections of *The Stone Princess* that appear in this story.

Speaking of brief appearances, *I Married the Duke*, the first book in my Prince Catchers series, which tells the story of Arabella and Luc's romance, prominently features Cam, including Cam and Jacqueline's introduction at the chateau (at which Jacqueline is pretty much struck dumb, which I would have been in her shoes too, so I don't blame her a bit). Another character fleetingly mentioned here, the mysterious rabble-rouser Lady Justice whose pamphlets are published by Brittle & Sons, plays a central role in my Falcon Club series. For more information about my books, including how they're all connected, as well as deleted scenes and giveaways, please visit my website at www.KatharineAshe.com. I love hearing from readers.

I offer special thanks for assistance with this book to angels Marcia Abercrombie and Mary Brophy Marcus, whose generosity is eclipsed only by their kindness and caring, and to Georgie C. Brophy and Bob Steeger for crucial last-minute assistance. Even when we're not working on a collaborative project, Caroline Linden, Maya Rodale and Miranda Neville make writing fiction more fun than it already is, and I am deeply glad for their friendship. For my agent, Kimberly Whalen, I am ever-grateful, as well as for my wonderful editor, Lucia Macro, and the other fabulous people at Avon Books who work magic with my books, especially Nicole Fischer, Katie Steinberg, Gail Dubov, Shawn Nicholls and Pam Jaffee. To Kim Castillo of Author's Best Friend, who is beyond splendid, countless thank yous.

To my mother, my husband and my son: from the bottom of my heart I appreciate your infinite support and love. Last but never least, for my readers, who embrace the Christmas message of joy and love in this and all seasons, I give jubilant thanks.

Eager to learn how Arabella and Luc first met?
Don't miss

I MARRIED THE DUKE,

the first in Katharine Ashe's delicious new series,

THE PRINCE CATCHERS,

available now from Avon Books!
And read on for a sneak peek at

I ADORED A LORD,

the second delightful romance in

THE PRINCE CATCHERS series,

coming in summer 2014!

An Excerpt from

I ADORED A LORD

Laughter bubbled from the archway and candlelight danced toward them along the walls. Lord Vitor doused the lamp and drew her behind the iron grill.

"What are you—"

He shook his head and released her.

Light footsteps tripped along stone, and into the great medieval keep flew a lady wearing fluffy white froth followed by a gentleman with shirt points to his ears. Seeming to flee, the lady moved at a pace far too slow to outdistance the gentleman's determined strides.

"Oh, Signore Anders! You must not!"

"But my darling Miss Abraccia, I must."

Ravenna folded her arms. He had called her his darling only the night before.

Prickling with gooseflesh and shivering, she rubbed at her skin. Behind the rack of shields and swords and crossbows it was much colder than in the storage room. The muslin gown

Ann had lent her was practical for the party in the adjacent chamber, which was well heated by two modern fireplaces and many dancing people, but ridiculously unsuited to hiding anywhere else in the fortress.

The man beside her, however, seemed perfectly comfortable. This must be due to ... she had no idea. She knew little about Lord Vitor Courtenay, except that he was less devil-may-care than he pretended to be among others, and that the subtle knocking together of her knees beneath her tissue-thin skirts now had more to do with his proximity than with the cold. Absurdly, the recollection of his body atop hers in the stable came to her again, of his weight pressing her into the straw. He had not come close to her since.

Until now.

Now their arms nearly brushed—his muscular, defined by the fabric of his fine coat, and hers bared practically to the shoulder. His breathing was even and slow. Clearly this closeness did not affect him, despite his teasing on the hillside that he still wished to kiss her. An impromptu swim in a frigid river could cool the most insistent ardor, she supposed.

"Why are we hiding?" she said beneath the trill of Miss Abraccia's thoroughly insincere protests and Mr. Anders' wine-soaked assurances.

Lord Vitor cut her a Dark Look.

"They cannot hear me," she whispered. "Her giggles drown out all else."

A crease appeared between his brows and he seemed to study her face as sometimes he did, as though searching her features for an answer to a question he had not spoken. When he looked at her like this she did not feel the cold. She felt hot and unsteady. And ill.

She should have let him teach her to dance.

The thought came unbidden and unwelcome. She did not want to learn how to dance and she did not want him to touch her again. Even the caress of his gaze now was too much to bear.

Then, with a hooding of his eyes she had seen only once before, it dipped to her mouth as on that night in the stable.

"Why am I allowing my toes to grow numb one by one?" she made herself say. Anything to halt the painful pleasure of his gaze upon her. *Anything.* For it was painful, she understood now. When he looked at her like this, an unendurable sort of misery gathered in her chest and belly that she needed to escape. That was the reason she had fled the drawing room earlier, to avoid his dark eyes and to avoid touching him again. "So that I can watch Mr. Anders cajole Miss Abraccia into his arms, since he failed to cajole me?" she forced through her lips. "He believes he is a poet, but in truth he is a boy."

He glanced into the hall, and for an instant both pleasure and misery abated.

"Killers may wear masks." His voice was low.

She peeked through the grill, her breaths fogging on the steel breastplate before her. Miss Abraccia took another dainty step away from Mr. Anders. Then she reversed direction and fell against his chest with all evidence of submission.

Ravenna simply couldn't watch. It was too foolish. "And you know this because . . .?"

"Because I have worn such masks. But no longer." His eyes flickered with torchlight. "He failed?"

He was a *killer?* This man who had risked his life to save her from an icy river? The only man in the castle whom she was quite certain was not the murderer they sought? "He?"

Across the hall, Mr. Anders murmured to the lady.

A muscle in Lord Vitor's jaw flexed.

"*Him?*" Ravenna whispered.

He said nothing.

"Of course he failed," she said. "He is a sorry tease and I don't—"

"He failed." The words seemed to come from deep in his chest. He looked up to the ceiling and then down at his feet and then finally, as though reluctantly, again at her mouth. "Would I fail?" His voice was unmistakably husky.

Ravenna's stomach clenched. He was not teasing now—not as he had at other times. He meant this question and he wanted an answer. She should slap him. Without delay she should slip out of this concealed place and save herself from certain trouble. That would serve as a response well enough.

"Would you fail?" she only heard herself repeat.

He looked very serious. "No."

Beneath her skin she was hot and confused and—she realized now—wanting. She wanted him to touch her and she was terrified of it. "No?" she asked, the chill barely stirring between them.

"No," he said. "Unless you bite me again." Laughter glimmered in his eyes. Abruptly, Ravenna could breathe again.

Then his hand touched hers.

And breathing became a distant memory . . .

With the publication of her debut novel in 2010, Katharine Ashe earned a spot among the American Library Association's "New Stars of Historical Romance." Amazon awarded *How to Be a Proper Lady* a place among the Ten Best Books of 2012 in Romance, *When a Scot Loves a Lady* is a nominee for the 2013 Library of Virginia Literary Award in Fiction, and in 2011 Katharine won the coveted Reviewers' Choice Award for *Captured by a Rogue Lord*. Reviewers call her books "breathtaking," "lushly intense" and "sensationally intelligent."

Katharine lives in the wonderfully warm Southeast with her beloved husband, son, dog, and a garden she likes to call romantic rather than unkempt. A professor of European history, she has made her home in California, Italy, France, and the northern United States. Please visit her website at www.KatharineAshe.com.

Visit www.AuthorTracker.com for exclusive information on your favorite HarperCollins authors.